KAYLA WREN

Knights of Winter

BLACK CHERRY
PUBLISHING

First published by Black Cherry Publishing 2020

Copyright © 2020 by Kayla Wren

This novel is entirely a work of fiction. The names, characters and incidents portrayed in it are the work of the author's imagination. Any resemblance to actual persons, living or dead, events or localities is entirely coincidental.

Kayla Wren asserts the moral right to be identified as the author of this work.

First edition

ISBN: 978-1-8381116-5-6

Cover art by JS Designs

This book was professionally typeset on Reedsy. Find out more at reedsy.com

Contents

Chapter 1

The wind billows into my hood and tears it back from my head. Icy sleet hammers my cheeks and eyes, droplets clinging to my glasses and making me half-blind. I yank my hood back up and hold it there, rain sliding down my wrist into my sleeve as I hurry across campus.

The clouds hang low overhead, dark gray and swollen, and street lamps glow orange even though it's barely 4pm. Laughter breaks out across the quad and I flinch, ducking my head.

I'm not a coward. But I'm too busy to stand up for myself right now. I have a list to check; plans to make; dreams to make real.

Those frat boys will have to entertain themselves for today. I angle myself away from them as I cross the paved courtyard, smiling in the depths of my hood.

I've waited months for this afternoon.

The automatic glass door to the History building shudders to the side as I approach. It's a cruel irony: the History department is housed in the most modern building on campus, a monstrosity of glass and steel. It's all straight lines and sharp edges; no mystery, no heart.

I mentioned it to one of the professors once, and he blinked around the lecture hall like he'd never seen it before.

The Mathematics department, meanwhile, is in a listed colonial brownstone. Go figure.

Warm, stale air washes over me as I squelch into the lobby. I let my hood drop, shaking out my head and arms like a dog. Raindrops shower onto the glossy black tiles, and steam creeps around the edge of my glasses.

Another laugh breaks out somewhere down the nearest corridor and I jerk, heart thumping. Flattening a palm on my chest, I will my racing heart to calm down as I drift out of the lobby towards Professor Walsh's office. It's late afternoon in the history department, not midnight in a graveyard.

Besides, there's nothing these assholes can say to me that they haven't said before. Sticks and stones, and all that. I gust out a long breath and wander down the long corridor.

There. I walked a mile in the rain to see this: a sheet of A4 paper tacked to Professor Walsh's office door, ink smudged and corners curling. He could have sent an email, of course, but that's not Walsh's style. Tradition over convenience, never mind the icy December rain.

I may be a history nerd, but at least I've embraced modern technology.

The paper taunts me from half the corridor away, a pale, blurry rectangle against the wood of the door. I pull my glasses off as I approach, wiping them with the cloth I keep tucked in my pocket, then sliding them back on my nose.

It's a short list. Only six names, even though over eighty students applied.

And who wouldn't? A funded trip to a legendary castle, half the world away? The chance to page through books in ancient libraries and sleep in the same rooms where historical figures once slept?

I scan the list, my heart leaping into my throat at the fifth name.

Gigi Russell.

"Yes!" I hiss, pumping the air. "Hell yes."

"Steady on, Gigi," a voice drawls behind my shoulder. "You're practically cursing."

Just like that, my soaring mood falters. I purse my lips and turn around.

Lance Lockford smirks down at me, his tawny hair slick with rain. It slides down his temples, down the pale column of his throat, and disappears into the neckline of his sweatshirt.

"My eyes are up here, you know."

I jerk my gaze back up to his, heat prickling over my cheeks. He always does this, always makes me tongue-tied and stupid. Teasing me is one of Lance Lockford's favorite games.

"What do you want, Lockford?"

Lance rolls his eyes and steps forward, crowding me back against the office door. He lifts one hand, and for a ridiculous moment, I think he's going to stroke my cheek or play with my hair. He does that sometimes. Pets a stray curl, or chucks me under the chin. I hate those moments and yearn for them in equal measure.

My mouth drops open, and I blink up at him with my chest heaving beneath the sodden bundle of my scarf. With his hair wet, I can smell the faint scent of his shampoo.

Lance reaches past me and taps a finger against the sheet of paper. He traces the list, his finger dragging over the names.

"Perfect." He smirks at my flushed cheeks as I glower up at him, disappointed. "All my favorite people on one trip."

No. I whirl around, my elbow catching him in the side. He

grunts and steps back as I read the list again.

I'd been so focused on finding my own name, I hadn't properly read the others.

Lance Lockford, Asher Penderly and his sister Melissa.

The three people I try most to avoid.

Not because they're cruel, like the frat boys, but because the sight of the three of them together leaves me hollow. They're so comfortable. So intimate. All inside jokes and casual touches.

I don't remember the last physical contact I had that wasn't a handshake.

Plus there's Lance's teasing, and Asher's kind smiles that crinkle his eyes at the corners...

"You can't," I mumble, lips numb.

"Can't what?" Lance snaps, annoyed now. "Can't go on a college trip because Freaky Gigi says so?"

I breathe hard, fogging up my own glasses, and step to one side, shaking my head. I don't look at Lance. I don't have my features under control.

"You don't even like this class." I sound strangled. "None of you do. You missed half the lectures."

"Keeping tabs on us, were you?"

I swallow and jerk my head again, even though the answer is yes. Whenever they're near, I can't tear my eyes away. And whenever they're gone, I feel a soothing, dull relief.

This can't be happening. I can't win a place on the trip of a lifetime, then ruin it before we've even gone.

I turn to Lance, eyes pleading.

"We were supposed to be chosen based on grades."

The last dregs of humor drain from his face, leaving him colder than the December sleet. When Lance speaks, he spits each word at me.

"Just because we're not weird and friendless doesn't mean we're fucking stupid."

I flinch. It's so much worse coming from him. Lance is moodier than the other two, yes, with a frown that settles over his brow when he thinks no one is looking. But as soon as there are people around, he's all cocky smiles and teasing jokes. I always try to sit out of his eye line but within earshot, so I can hear the steady stream of his one liners.

The class entertainer.

He's not laughing now.

"That's not what I meant," I whisper, but it's too late. Lance turns on his heel and strides away.

I know the trio are all smart. But really, all three of them winning a place? After their attendance was so poor?

It's statistically highly unlikely. That's all I meant to say.

I turn back to read the list a final time, chewing on my bottom lip. This, right here, is why I'm better off alone. Even when I like someone, even when I mean well, I screw it all up. It's like everyone else got a secret script when they were growing up—a How To for social interaction.

I close my eyes and thump my forehead against the door.

Freaky Gigi strikes again.

* * *

My first hour on British soil is a blur of cheesy airport posters, lines of grumpy travelers, and the dull roar of hand dryers behind closed bathroom doors.

Our plane touches down just as the sun slips below the horizon, staining the miles of tarmac red. I'm the only one in our row awake to see it—Annabelle, another girl from our class, snores in the seat next to mine, her head tipped back and her mouth wide open. On her other side, an exchange student called Thabo dozes in the aisle seat, a scarf wrapped around his face up to his eyebrows.

The trio are in the row behind us; Professor Walsh and his grad student Morgan are in the row in front. The back of my neck prickled the entire flight, itching under Lance Lockford's scrutiny.

He hates me now. This always happens. I unhinge my jaw, stuff my whole foot in my mouth, and an acquaintance becomes an enemy.

Annabelle grunts, shuffling in her seat, her elbow nudging mine off the armrest. I sigh, the stale airplane air too thin in my lungs, and stare back out the window.

Outside on the runway, dozens of workers in neon yellow jackets swarm over the cooling plane. The seat belt light dings off, the engine dies, and hundreds of creaky passengers grumble and scrabble around for their things.

Morgan's head pops over the seat in front of Annabelle, glancing at the two sleepers before shooting me a quick smile. He's only a few years older than us, in his late twenties, with neat black hair and smoky grey eyes behind his glasses. I've never seen Superman, but I imagine Morgan would make one hell of a Clark Kent.

"Not long now. Make sure you have everything."

I nod, but keep my mouth shut.

Since the blow up with Lance, I've renewed my focus on improving my social skills. The surest way I've found to avoid causing offense is to not speak in the first place.

It's been a long couple of weeks. I'm starting to forget what my voice sounds like.

Morgan's smile fades as he watches me, waiting for me to speak. When I stare back at him, silent and exhausted, he presses his lips together and spins back around in his seat.

Is that bad? For God's sake. I'm damned if I do, damned if I don't. I need a manual.

Or better yet, I need a distraction. Worn tapestries and cold flagstones. I'll have so much more to say to everyone once we reach Cariadon Castle.

We stumble like zombies through the airport corridors, past floor to ceiling posters of English cities. London; Bristol; Manchester. Bright lights and cherry red buses.

Where we're going couldn't be more different. I hug my arms around my waist, my backpack digging into my shoulders. My preliminary research into the Welsh mountains promised stark landscapes and bitter cold.

I have my thermal long johns. I can't wait.

My bag is one of the first to slide onto the carousel. I heave my father's old tartan suitcase off the conveyor belt, turning pink under Lance's gaze. He watches me, arms crossed and jaw clenched, as I lug the suitcase onto the ground. My glasses slide to the tip of my nose, wobbling over the expanse of thin air, and I push them back up just in time.

"For fuck's sake…" I hear Lance mutter, but when I glance over he's staring at the carousel. Next to him, Melissa catches my eye, frowning at me as she chews the inside of her cheek.

She looks so fresh. Like she somehow had a full night's sleep and a shower while the rest of us squashed ourselves into that tin can. Her platinum blond hair is in two French braids; her makeup flawless.

I offer a smile. Melissa rolls her eyes and turns away.

Right. They've decided they hate me.

I yank the handle on my suitcase out and drag it on wobbly wheels towards the edge of the room. As I pass the trio, Melissa reaches out and pinches my sleeve between her thumb and forefinger.

I pause. "Yes?"

Melissa cocks her head to the side. When she leans in, her breath smells like spearmint.

"Lance told us what you said, Gigi. You know, you're not half as smart as you think you are."

This is probably something we can agree on, so I shrug.

"I expect you're right."

Melissa's mouth tightens. It was the wrong thing to say. Her grip tightens on my sleeve, and she yanks me close.

"Say shit like that to him again, and I don't care how freaky you are. I'll make you fucking sorry."

I peel her off my sleeve one finger at a time, catching Lance's eye over her shoulder as I do it. He's talking to Asher, but when his gaze finds mine, he doesn't look away.

"I'm already fucking sorry," I say, loud enough for them both to hear. I don't curse often, but there's a certain harsh pleasure to it. A tiny thrill. I must integrate more curse words into my daily vocabulary.

Melissa and Lance both scoff, but I've had enough. They don't want to listen, only to talk. I wheel my suitcase past them, bumping the wheel over Melissa's foot.

* * *

Forty seven minutes later, my back rests against the scuffed wall of the baggage claim as my ass goes numb on the floor. I rest my ancient laptop on my crossed legs, a drafted email to my parents typed on the smudgy screen.

I squint at what I've written so far, my mouth twisted into a grimace.

Dear Mother and Father...

I jab the backspace key.

Hi, Mom and Dad!

That's better. Perky. Like something a normal daughter would write. I blow my bangs off my forehead, typing furiously as I edit myself to sound halfway human. I prefer writing to speaking, but even in an email, I come across so stiff and formal—like a poorly disguised cyborg in a sci-fi movie.

Distantly, I hear Professor Walsh berating the airport staff. All of our bags have emerged except Annabelle's, and I guess we can't leave without it. Annabelle herself stands next to the empty carousel, her thin shoulders rigid as she watches the conveyor belt go round and round.

Sighing, I focus back on my email. I promised my parents biweekly communication, and already I regret such a lofty goal.

It's not like they even reply half the time. But my mind was fuzzy from Christmas day cocktails, and I let them trick me into an oath.

My eyes flick up from my screen in time to see Asher tip back his head and roar with laughter on the other side of the room. He punches Lance's shoulder, his friend's mouth quirking up at the side as he stumbles back half a step.

What I wouldn't give to make Asher Penderly laugh like that. To make anyone laugh like that.

As if he can feel my eyes on them, Lance suddenly scowls at where I've sat in the corner. I duck my head and tap random keys, trying and failing to keep the heat from my cheeks.

It was bad enough around the trio before, when I hadn't accidentally called them stupid. They barely acknowledged my existence, but that wasn't the problem—I appreciated that about them.

No: they make each other laugh like this. It aches to hear them. Makes me feel piercingly alone.

I still feel that way around them, but now they hate me too.

A knot forms in my chest as I sit there, blindly staring at my laptop screen. I tap at random keys, typing gibberish, then give myself a mental kick. Screw this.

I slam my laptop shut and jolt to my feet, shoving it into my backpack. My ankle boots squeak on the linoleum as I hurry over to Professor Walsh.

"Professor?"

He stands with Morgan by the baggage carousel, an old-fashioned leather trunk at his feet. Professor Walsh is a man who has seen too many Indiana Jones films. He dresses like he's just got back from the field, in tight waistcoats and shirtsleeves—never mind that he works behind a desk. He's handsome, I guess, for his forty-something years, but that hasn't done his personality any favors.

Plus, his breath always reeks of stale coffee. I lean back an inch when he turns to me, his muggy breath wafting over my face.

"What, girl?" He sees it's me and huffs. "This is not the time, Gigi."

I force my lips into a smile. Not far away, I can feel the trio's eyes on me, and my heart patters faster.

"I understand. I just have a quick question—"

"Not now!" he thunders, spittle landing on my cheek. I rear back, meeting Morgan's wide eyes before I spin on my heel and leave.

Normal people right now might laugh it off. Or skulk away to a corner to lick their wounds.

I can't. I snatch my suitcase from the pile of group luggage and stride across the wide hall. Behind me, someone calls my name, but I don't stop when I reach the doorway to customs, nor the arrivals lobby with its lines of cab drivers holding signs.

I wheel all the way to the automatic doors and out into the frozen January night.

Air. I need air. In the darkness, where no one can see me.

* * *

"Gigi!"

Several feet away, Morgan barges out of the airport and onto the sidewalk. His head darts left and right, taking in the line of boxy black London cabs and the city bus groaning to a halt at its stop.

"Shit." His shoulders drop, a pale hand raking through his hair. From my spot against the wall, tucked in the shadows, I can see the slight tremble in his fingers under the glow of the fluorescent signs.

I clear my throat, swiping at my cheeks with the tail of my scarf. I've already made enough of a scene, crashing out here like an elephant through the undergrowth.

Even so, my voice comes out strange when I call out to Morgan. Kind of warbly.

"Over here."

He jerks around, eyes narrowing as he scans the shadows clinging to the side of the building. I raise a mitten, and he latches onto the movement, relief spreading over his face.

"You shouldn't wander off. Airports can be dangerous places."

He steps closer but stops a few feet away. Like he doesn't want to spook me.

"I know."

I *did* know. I read the UN's report on Human Trafficking before I left. I knew full well I was being an idiot when I stormed off all alone, but the thought of staying in that room with all those eyes on me, after everyone heard the way Professor Walsh yelled—

"I'm sorry. Sometimes I just get…"

I trail off. How many people have I tried to explain this to before? And how many people stuck around?

Difficult, Mom calls me. *Hard work.*

But Morgan's mouth quirks up on one side.

"Overwhelmed?" he offers. I'm nodding hard before he even finishes the word.

"Yes. I get overwhelmed." He's still standing there, like he's waiting for me to keep talking. So, for once, I do. "It's the noises, or something. I can't filter things out. I notice every sound and sight and smell, and then when something extra happens on top—something like Professor Walsh—it's too much. I have to get away."

Morgan hums, stepping closer. The neon glow of the airport signs washes up and over his face, then he's plunged into the shadows with me.

"It's not uncommon, you know."

I shrug. Sure seems like everyone else can handle these things.

"Have you been to a doctor?"

I glare at his shape in the dark.

"I'm not sick."

"I never said you were."

We fall into awkward silence. I shift on my suitcase, my weight making it creak, and I suddenly wish Morgan would leave. It was nice to talk to him for a moment—the knot in my chest has eased, and I can breathe better now. But I don't want to entertain him. I don't want to have to be charming.

"I'm fine waiting alone. I won't leave this spot, I promise."

It's too dark to see Morgan's expression, but his voice sounds careful.

"We're responsible for you, Gigi..."

I snort. "I'm twenty years old. I can get married, get a tattoo, enlist in the military, and open a credit card. All in one day, if I'm feeling industrious. I think I can sit on my suitcase out here for twenty minutes."

Morgan chuckles. "Fair point. Do you have your phone?"

I unlock it and hand it over without a word. My contact list has my parents, the student office, and campus security. Morgan frowns down at the screen, the blue light reflected on his glasses as he tries to keep scrolling, before it finally sinks in.

Mercifully, he doesn't say anything. He enters his number and hands the phone back.

"In case you need me."

My throat tightens, but I manage a nod. His footsteps clip against the concrete as he walks back to the entrance.

I sink against the chilled brick, strands of my hair catching on the stone. I turn my phone over in my hands, then unlock the screen again.

My contacts screen glows up at me, one number longer.

Morgan. *In case you need me.*

13

Chapter 2

We load onto a minibus three hours behind schedule, without Annabelle's bag. Morgan slides into the driver's seat, humming and nodding as Professor Walsh rants in his ear about the shitty airport and shitty customer service and shitty, shitty Britain.

Professor Walsh is not a serene man.

The rest of us load up our cases and climb the steps into the bus. Thabo slides into the first seat he reaches and immediately falls comatose. Annabelle sits next to him, eyes lined with exhaustion. She reminds me of a ballet teacher I had when I was young—she has the same olive skin, the same curly black hair. She even has the same vacant despair in her eyes when I stop to talk to her.

I purse my lips, scanning Annabelle's height and approximate size.

"You can share my things if you like," I blurt.

She blinks up at me in surprise. Behind me, Melissa and Lance bitch loudly about how I'm holding up the line.

I ignore them, gazing down at Annabelle with my eyebrows raised.

"We're approximately the same size. You're a little thinner, but that should work in your favor."

Annabelle frowns at me, shakes her head like she's trying to clear it, then offers up a shaky smile.

"Sure, Gigi. That would be great, thank you."

I nod, relieved, and march down the bus, ready to get away from everyone and everything. Unfortunately, there are boxes of supplies stacked up on the spare rows, forcing us all to share.

Yet another injustice on this very trying day.

I throw myself down in a window seat, stuffing my backpack between my feet. Lance slides into the row opposite, craning his neck to stare into the darkness outside. Melissa sits beside him, smiling nastily when she catches me staring.

I pluck at a loose thread on my mitten, my tangled hair falling into a curtain and cutting me off from them.

"Is this seat taken?"

Asher rests his hand on the headrest, his wide mouth curved into its perpetual smile. His blond hair skims the collar of his coat, and a dimple puckers his cheek.

I shrug, shuffling closer to the window.

It's the last free seat. It's not like I could turn him away, no matter how much Melissa glares. If she didn't want me by either her brother or Lance, she should have sucked it up and sat by me herself.

Asher grins and lowers himself into the seat, unperturbed by my lack of social skills. He keeps one leg stretched into the aisle, folding the rest of his long limbs to make himself fit.

"I've never been to Europe."

He chats so easily. So confident that the other person wants to hear it. I tug on my loose thread, more viciously than before.

"And this castle, Jesus. Did you look it up before we left?"

I huff. "Of course."

What am I, an idiot? I'm hardly going to waste this once in

15

a lifetime opportunity by not bothering to prepare. There's a folder on my laptop dedicated to background research and a thorough bibliography. It's backed up to the cloud.

"Right, right." Asher nudges me with his elbow. "I bet it's haunted."

I close my eyes and breathe in hard through my nose.

"While theoretically there may be some merit to paranormal investigations, if only to prove how *baseless* the theories are, I hardly think—"

Asher's hand closes over my mitten.

"I'm kidding, Gigi."

"Oh."

He doesn't move his hand. I can feel its warm weight through the scratchy wool. After a moment, I nudge him off, slide off my mitten, then place his palm back on my bare skin.

Satisfaction curls through me all the way to my toes. His calloused palm is warm and dry.

Asher chuckles in my ear, and I turn my head. Our noses are a few inches apart, his blue eyes dancing.

"You are full of surprises."

I gnaw on my lip.

"That's not always a good thing."

Asher shrugs, shuffling closer so his arm presses against mine. Even through both our sweaters, I can feel the ridges of his muscles.

"I like surprises."

I catch sight of Melissa over his shoulder, her furious gaze burning into Asher's hand on mine. Automatically, I go to pull my hand away, but then I pause.

Why should I? I'm not doing anything wrong.

Instead, I flip my hand over and wind my fingers through

Asher's. His thumb strokes up mine, lingering on the knuckle. I melt back into my seat, away from Melissa's eyes, practically purring like a cat.

For such a hermit, I sure do love to be touched. I've suffered through many lackluster hookups just to feel the warmth of bare skin.

Asher Penderly puts them all to shame. I close my eyes, hunker down in my seat, and focus on the sweep of his thumb over my hand.

* * *

We pull into our hotel in the middle of the night. Our tires crunch over a long gravel drive, the minibus lurching, and Asher rouses me from where I've fallen asleep on his shoulder.

"Gigi. Hey, Gigi. We're here."

I squint at him, bleary eyed, swiping the drool from my chin. There's definitely a wet patch on his sweater.

"Already?"

Asher chuckles.

"We've been driving over six hours. You fell asleep in the first twenty minutes."

"Huh."

I never sleep in transit. The constant noise from whatever vehicle I'm on; the sickly, swaying motion—usually I'm lucky if I can make it through a trip without vomiting.

Six hours of uninterrupted sleep on Asher Penderly's shoulder? That's... unexpected.

We spill one by one onto the gravel, lining up to unload our bags. We're all clumsy and quiet, maybe from fatigue, or maybe we're all daunted by the mountains rising up on all sides. The

17

night is absolute: inky blackness with the pinpricks of bright stars. No city lights to dull their shine out here—the milky way swirls overhead, between the silhouettes of mountain peaks.

The guest house nestles in a dip between two slopes. Lanterns light the path to the doorway, and a wooden sign hangs overhead, creaking in the breeze. The words 'Castle Inn' are etched into the wood, along with a rudimentary carving of a turret.

A shiver runs up my spine. We're so close. This same breeze has wound around the great walls of Cariadon Castle. It's tugged at the grass and gorse.

"They're eerie, aren't they? The mountains."

Morgan stands at my side, a duffel bag slung over one shoulder. We cluster around the doorway as Professor Walsh slams the knocker, muttering to himself about the basic rules of customer service.

"I suppose they are." I glance around again, the icy breeze tugging on the ends of my hair. "I expect it's normal to feel unsettled in a land with so much history. Just think how much these mountains have seen; how many bones are buried beneath the grass."

"You're a fucking cheery pair," Lance mutters, dropping his bag on Morgan's other side. "Tone it down a bit, will you? Freaky Gigi doesn't need any encouragement."

Morgan bristles next to me, but it's Asher's voice that cuts through the night air.

"Don't call her that."

Asher pushes next to Lance, his mouth set in a rare frown. Lance blinks at him, his gaze darting to me, then he shuts his jaw with a click.

"It doesn't bother me," I tell Asher, reasonably confident it's

18

not a lie. "I've been called far worse."

Asher turns his frown on me.

"All the more reason for him to cut it the fuck out."

Morgan grumbles in agreement, but the front door finally swings open. I'm saved from this social minefield by an elderly woman in a burgundy house coat.

"Well," she says, her accent lilting, "we thought you'd never show. You came this close to losing your rooms and sleeping out with the sheep."

Professor Walsh splutters, his face turning red, but she's already turned away. She leads us inside, lining us up against the stone wall.

"Boots off."

Professor Walsh rallies. "How ridiculous. We've paid for these rooms—"

The woman cuts him off, holding up a gnarled hand.

"I'll not sweep these floors three times a day when you can just take off your boots. The shoe racks are by the wall. Now: off."

I catch Annabelle's eye and we both smother a grin. Professor Walsh is a well-known tyrant, always throwing his power around, and since his outburst in the airport I'm practically giddy watching this old lady smack him down.

"Come on." Morgan steps in before Professor Walsh can rupture a vein. He toes his own boots off, gesturing for the rest of us to follow his example.

The woman huffs. "At least one of you has some manners."

It's a shame we're only staying one night. I like it here.

* * *

The lumpy twin mattress digs into my spine. Every time I roll over, a musical chorus of bed springs sing out, cutting through the silent inn.

I wince, settling on my right side again for the third time in a few minutes. For hours, it's been like this. Despite the pitch black sky outside, and the owl hooting outside in the sparse trees, I am wide awake. As far as my body is concerned, I just had a full night's sleep mashed up against Asher's shoulder.

I grunt, flopping onto my back and staring up at the beams. Without my glasses, the lines of the dark wood are fuzzy in the gloom. I raise one arm overhead, pointing as I trace the contours of my ceiling.

"For God's sake."

I drop my hand to the mattress and breathe out hard. I did not fly halfway around the world—crossing my first ocean—to lie here in the dark with my thoughts. I snatch my glasses from the side table and roll out of bed, the bed springs shrieking, and throw a sweater over my pajamas. After stuffing my feet into thick socks and shrugging on my coat, I tiptoe out of the room.

The flagstones are freezing beneath my feet, their chill seeping through my socks. My teeth are chattering by the time I cram my feet into my boots, hopping around in the deserted hallway. Through the windows, blue predawn light washes over the hills. It's not enough to dampen the stars, but it's enough for me to pick out the paintings hung on the whitewashed walls.

Bare, rugged landscapes. Scraggly sheep and tumbledown barns. I gaze at each frame as I wander through the halls, my illicit boots soft on the stone.

There's a reading room. An old-fashioned breakfast parlor

crowded with tables. A rickety cabinet with a guest book full of scrawled reviews.

I look around, but there's no pen. I grin to myself. Seems the old lady likes to supervise her reviews.

I find the door to the gardens at the back of the inn. It's down another stone corridor, empty except for a mahogany cabinet filled with china plates.

The lock turns easily in my hand. Jackpot.

Full daylight won't come for a few hours yet—not in winter. But there's enough of a glow to see the heather and bracken coating the slopes on either side, along with the occasional white flash of a sheep. The wet scent of earth and a hint of wood smoke carry on the breeze, and I wander down a dirt path, sucking it all into my lungs.

The end of a cigarette flares red overhead. I leap back, heart pounding in my chest, and find three pale faces watching me from the woodshed roof.

"Good morning."

Asher's voice is warm. Everything Lance and Melissa's faces are not.

"Um." I unstick my tongue from the roof of my mouth. "Hi."

"Come join us, Gigi."

Asher offers a hand to me, leaning over the roof edge. I can see how they got up there now: the woodpile, then the upturned barrel, and the roof as the landing area.

Melissa scoffs quietly behind him, but Asher ignores her, leaning down another inch.

I step closer, glancing at the slippery woodpile; the moss on the barrel.

"All right."

Asher's eyebrows go up, his smile stretching wide. I take

21

his hand, his fingers firm on mine, and scramble up onto the barrel.

"Um." I pause with the roof at chest height, Asher's hand still tight around mine. "My upper body strength leaves a lot to be desired."

Lance mutters something under his breath, but shuffles to the edge next to Asher. He takes my other hand, and between the two of them, I'm pulled easily onto the roof.

"Thank you." I crawl away from the edge on wobbly legs. "You're very strong." I turn around and sit, catching a shared glance between Asher and Lance. "What?"

A sickly feeling slides through me. I don't dare look at Melissa.

If they didn't want me up here, why did they ask? Why make everything so damn hard to navigate? I swallow hard, readying myself to shuffle back the way I came.

But Asher shakes his head, his eyes crinkling as he smiles.

"Nothing. We're glad you're here, Gigi."

It's definitely presumptuous of Asher to speak for the others, but I believe him at least. And Lance and Melissa wouldn't hate me so much if I hadn't accidentally called them idiots.

"Me too." I smile at them all, practicing my eye contact. Melissa looks sour, but Lance gives me a brief nod.

"Here." He thrusts the cigarette towards me. "You might as well."

I sniff, and a much earthier smell than tobacco fills my nose. After all the endless high school workshops and anti-drug campaigns, I'm almost relieved to finally face the peer pressure everyone promised. After my first year at college, I worried it would never happen.

"Yes," I say decisively, taking the joint from Lance. Our

fingers brush, and his brown eyes meet mine. "I agree. I might as well."

Asher lets out a shocked laugh, and I grin at him before taking a drag. I pinch the joint between my finger and thumb, just like they do in the movies.

"I don't feel anything," I cough out after holding the smoke in my lungs.

Lance winks, the warmest he's been in weeks.

"Give it a minute."

We sit for what feels like hours, bundled up in coats and scarves on top of the woodshed. It's not too high, but from up here we can see the exact moment when the sky tinges pink. There's the dull thud of hooves on rock, and when we crane our necks, there are wild ponies picking their way through the bracken.

"Wow." I'm talking mostly to myself, like usual, but the others murmur in agreement. I bury my nose in my scarf, eyes watering from the cold, and try to soak in every sight and sound.

For once, I'm not blocking things out. I want it all.

I absorb it too, every last detail, right down to the feel of Lance's palm against mine as he lowers me back down onto the barrel. He has broad hands, with square knuckles, and for a bizarre moment I want to lick his wrist.

"Thank you," I mumble instead, and set back off towards the inn before he can see my face.

"No worries, Gigi," I hear him mutter at my back. He sounds tired. He should have slept longer.

I don't say so, because it's none of my business, and because the clink of china is seeping through the windows to the breakfast room. I duck through the back door and hurry to

23

my room, kicking my boots off as I go.

* * *

"I have something for you."

I dig my spoon into my muesli, ignoring the chatter around me. This was supposed to be a healthy food choice, and there are certainly nutritious ingredients in my bowl, but God—at what cost? My nose wrinkles as I chew on another mouthful, grinding away at the tasteless mush.

At least I will have something positive to report to my parents. I don't believe in deception as a rule, but I don't think I'll mention my first experience of marijuana. Our communications are strained at the best of times.

"Gigi."

I glance up, grimacing as I chew. Morgan stands over me, his gray eyes sparkling with amusement. His shirtsleeves are rolled to the elbow, and his top two buttons are undone. The edges of his collarbone poke out from beneath the material.

My mouth goes impossibly drier.

"There are other food options, you know."

With a great effort, I swallow.

"I am aware." I snatch up my apple juice and down half the glass before putting it back on the table with a thud. Annabelle and Thabo look over from the next table, and I give them a halfhearted wave.

The tables are all for two. My stomach clenched when we filed in here and saw them. Annabelle sat with Thabo; Professor Walsh with Morgan; Asher with his sister. Lance walked in and took one look at me, then dragged a chair next to Melissa.

It doesn't matter. The way this muesli is fighting back, I could hardly keep up a conversation.

Still, I will admit to myself that sitting alone stings more than usual. I suppose this morning's interlude on the wood shed gave me false hope.

"Here."

Morgan thrusts a paper folder under my nose. I take it, thumbing through the pages as he slides into the chair opposite me.

I frown at the text, trying to concentrate, but it's difficult when Morgan is clearly fresh from the shower. His skin is scrubbed and clean, the scent of soap on the air, and his dark hair is damp and curling. I want to bury my nose in it and inhale. I want to wind it around my fingers.

"Well?" He sounds eager. "I really think you should go for this, Gigi."

I blink and refocus on the papers in my hand. A call for papers… open submissions… Celtic legends and history…

The papers crinkle as my hand clenches, and I force my fingers to relax, placing the folder on the breakfast table and smoothing down the creases.

"I'm an undergraduate student."

Morgan smiles. "Yes, I had noticed. It's open to all."

"I've never written a paper like that."

"I've read your other work. You could if you tried."

I chew on my lip, trying and failing to be the voice of reason. Applying for opportunities like this, submitting academic papers—it is certainly in my detailed career plan, but it's scheduled for several years away.

Is Morgan right? Could I really do this now?

"Don't fill her head with that, Morgan." Professor Walsh

glowers down at us both, toast crumbs dusting his waistcoat. "There's no time for independent research on this trip."

I stiffen in my wooden chair.

"What about in my personal time?"

Professor Walsh levels me a look. "Yes, I suppose you'll have plenty of that."

He means my solo breakfast. My lack of friends. The way he always needs to assign someone to work with me on group projects—never mind that I inevitably end up doing all the work.

I swallow and look down at my food, prodding a raisin with my spoon.

Morgan says something, his tone clipped, but I block it out. I close my eyes and breathe in through my nose, pushing away the clink of spoons on china and the hiss of the kettle and the tap of tree branches on the window.

When I open my eyes again, the barrage of sounds rushes back in, but I'm ready. I look up at Professor Walsh.

"I'll work on it privately." I speak over whatever Morgan's saying, cutting him off. "It won't affect you, Professor."

He grunts, eyes flicking over my wild hair and patterned woolly sweater.

"See that it doesn't."

Morgan waits until the professor has ducked through the breakfast room doorway before he leans closer, his hand twitching towards mine. He snatches it back before it touches my skin, but I watch the near-miss with interest.

"Ignore him, Gigi. You don't need his permission anyway."

I smile. Morgan really is lovely first thing in the morning.

"You know, you could be on television. In an advert for breakfast cereal or something. Like a handsome single father feeding his children before school."

A faint blush creeps over Morgan's cheeks, and he sits back. His hands drop off the table completely.

"Thank you for the details." I scoop the folder off the table and stand. "Perhaps I could show you my outline before I begin writing?"

Morgan nods, still mute.

I wink at a staring Lance on my way out.

Chapter 3

Cariadon Castle is only accessible by foot. It's deep in the mountains, through forests and valleys. When I read about the trek awaiting us, I immediately started wearing my new hiking boots around my dorm room to break them in.

I'm not overly athletic, but for Cariadon Castle, I would undergo a grueling training regime.

Fortunately, that's not necessary. It's a single day's hike, and while it's on a steep incline, we only need to take backpacks with a week's worth of supplies. I hoist my backpack onto my shoulders, rethinking the ancient laptop weighing down my bag for the millionth time.

No. We're here to study, to research, to learn. I won't hinder myself because I'm afraid of aching muscles.

"Stay together," Morgan calls out as we gather at the edge of the tree line. Our suitcases will be stored at the inn; a privilege which Morgan charmed for us after Professor Walsh insulted the owner again.

"If you need to stop, say so. Everybody pick one person; if that person falls behind or wanders out of sight, it's on you to alert the group."

Everyone smiles and nudges each other. I scrape at the pine

needles coating the dirt with my boot. I don't need anyone to pick me, anyway. I'm not stupid enough to wander off in a strange forest.

"We'll be stopping for lunch and for water breaks. Keep an eye out for historical features in the trees—the British isles are riddled with burial cairns and standing stones."

I perk up at that, and Morgan shoots me a wink. Warmth unfurls in my chest and spreads through my limbs, and I can't help the smug smile on my face when Lance turns around to frown at me.

I shrug at him, then turn back to Morgan. I don't know what's sexier—seeing him be all bossy and in charge, or the knowledge that we're only one day away from the castle.

"All right. Move out!"

We fall into single file to begin with, the dirt path through the trees too narrow to clump together in groups. I find myself directly behind Asher, his blue and gray backpack lurching as he walks. His legs are so long, I take two steps for every one of his strides, and I fight to keep myself from gasping for breath too shamelessly.

It's harder going than it looks, walking up a mountainside.

The trees are a mix of different types, some bare branches stripped for winter while others bristle with dark green needles. Bracken coats the ground, fronds whispering against our pant legs as we walk past, and clusters of white mushrooms sprout from tree trunks and fallen logs.

It's quiet. There's the thud of our feet, dead leaves and pine cones crackling beneath our boots, and our quickened breaths. Bird cries thrill through the trees, and squirrels skitter up and down the bark, tails bobbing. But there's no roar of traffic, no beep of electronics.

Just the forest, the sounds of our progress, and the trickle of a nearby stream.

"You still there, Gigi?"

The sound of Asher's voice cutting through the quiet makes me jump. I stumble, kicking a small rock to the side.

"Of course I'm still here. Why?"

Asher turns and grins at me over his shoulder, still walking. The breeze whistling through the trees tugs at his blond hair.

"Because you're my person. You heard what Morgan said. I need to keep an eye on you."

I watch the back of his head doubtfully as he walks on. We can partner if Asher likes, but I wouldn't be my own first choice for mountain rescue.

It's nice he thought of me, though. I breathe a little easier as we forge up the slope.

* * *

We stop for our first water break when the path bursts into a clearing. Mossy boulders crest through the bracken, and the stream we've been following gathers in a crystal clear pool.

Asher bends over the water, scooping a handful up and splashing it over his face. Lance scoffs and Asher straightens up, grinning, shaking his hair like a wet dog. I chew on my lip as I approach, my cheeks red and sweaty from walking for hours.

"A lot of the pools around here have legends attached." They both turn to me, and I clear my throat, mentally kicking myself for interrupting. "Things like spirits who live in the water, or secret cities at the bottom of a lake. Monsters and magic. That sort of thing."

"I thought you were a scholar," Asher says, teasing. "Don't tell me you believe in magic, Gigi?"

I shake my head. "No. I believe in stories, though. You can learn a lot about history and cultures from the legends they told. King Arthur, for example—"

I cut off, flushing, when I notice several faces staring at me.

"Go on," Asher says after a moment. He gives a slight smile. "It's interesting."

I breathe out in a gust. "Well, there are loads of stories about him. Excalibur and Camelot, yes, but also accounts with verifiable dates and places. He was a real, flesh and blood man who was made into a legend."

Melissa drops her backpack next to Lance with a thump, swigging from a water bottle. When she's done, she wipes her mouth on the back of her hand and looks me straight in the eye.

"Is this your version of flirting? Because it's painful to watch."

Lance snorts, and even Asher lets a grin skate over his face before he smooths out his features.

It's too late, though. I know what I saw.

I turn away without another word, grabbing my backpack and retreating to the other side of the clearing. Asher calls after me, but I block it out. He's white noise, along with the rest.

I drop my backpack by a boulder and scramble up, cushioned by the moss. I'm all set to spend the rest of the break alone, blocking bad thoughts and soaking in my surroundings. But a pair of hands grip onto the boulder beside me and a brown head of hair pops up.

"Move over a bit."

I shuffle to the side as Annabelle pulls herself up. She's a

31

lot more agile than me, her shoulders strong. She settles next to me, brushing stray hairs out of her face and shooting me a quick smile.

"It's beautiful here, isn't it?"

I run the question through my brain, searching for traps and hidden meanings.

"…Yes," I say, after a moment, still unsure. "It is."

Annabelle leans back on her palms, kicking the heels of her boots against the boulder. She's wearing a pair of my thermal leggings and an old sweatshirt from Dad's college days.

"Thanks again for the clothes."

"No problem."

We fall into silence. I bite my lip

Goddamn it. I'm so bad at this.

After a moment, I'm ready to try again. I've run my sentence through my mind, and I'm ninety percent certain that it won't cause offense.

"You were very unlucky. To lose all your things."

Annabelle shrugs. "It's just stuff. I was mostly worried about stinking for weeks." She prods me with her elbow. "You solved that for me."

I straighten up an inch higher on my boulder.

"I'm nicer than people realize."

Annabelle lays a hand on my forearm.

"People are idiots, Gigi. Who gives a shit what they think?"

I've privately had those thoughts plenty of times, but I figured I must be missing something. If Annabelle thinks so too, though—well, why should I care at all?

I pat the back of Annabelle's hand.

"This has been an excellent discussion."

Annabelle laughs softly, the sound melting into the trickle

of the stream, and offers me her crumpled bag of trail mix. I rummage through for an attractive cashew as she nudges me again.

"Agreed."

* * *

I spend the rest of the hike to the castle walking near Thabo and Annabelle. They're funny together—they were strangers before this trip, but already they have inside jokes and a kind of code when they talk. Thabo is a year younger than the rest of us, but I learn during the lunch break that he speaks fourteen different languages.

A polyglot. Incredible. The human brain is a wonderful thing.

I tell him so, and Thabo throws back his head and laughs, his woolen beanie dropping to the carpet of pine needles behind him. A semester in blustery Llewellyn College did not prepare him for the January cold of the Welsh mountains. He's constantly burrowing deeper into his coat, wrapping his arms around himself.

I offered to lend him my mittens but he declined. It's reasonable. My hands are much smaller than his.

The first few hours of the hike were the worst, when our limbs were stiff and the blood sluggish in our veins. By the time we've covered a few miles, our strides lengthen and our muscles warm up. I savor the burn in my limbs and the whistle of fresh air through my lungs, studiously ignoring the trio walking behind me.

People are idiots. I do not care what they think.

Instead, I focus all my spare mental energy on the two non-

33

idiots by my side. They chatter about their course load for next semester, and about Thabo's plans to visit Ghana over the summer. And when it gets to be too much, I let my attention drift, and I watch Morgan's broad shoulders and narrow hips up ahead.

His long strides forge up the mountain path, his footsteps sure on the rocks.

I reach back and tug my water bottle free, taking a long swig. This is thirsty work.

When the afternoon light dims, I quicken my pace and join Morgan at the front of the line.

"Will we see it before the light's gone?"

Morgan frowns at the path ahead.

"We should do."

It's not a reassuring statement, and a bubble of anxiety swells in my chest. We need to see Cariadon Castle. I need to see it. Built into the mountainside and surrounded by trees—the view on the approach exactly as it was hundreds of years ago.

"If not today then tomorrow, Gigi."

I nod vaguely at Morgan. It's not good enough.

"Come on."

I grab Morgan's wrist and tug him forwards. I'd set off on my own but I don't know the way, and besides, I expect that would be what Mom calls a 'selfish impulse'. My glasses fog and my bangs stick to my forehead with sweat, but I tow Morgan along.

"All right, all right. Steady." Morgan extricates himself from my grasp. He slows down a tiny bit, but we keep going faster than before.

I grin at him, breathing hard. Morgan rolls his eyes but smiles back. We round a jagged outcropping of stone and stumble to a halt.

Cariadon Castle. I press my palm against my chest. Even through my layers, I can feel my heart pound.

It's not huge, as castles go. Nothing like the massive keeps dotted along the coastline. Cariadon Castle is only a little bigger than the Greek houses back on campus, its mossy stone walls blending into the landscape so well a plane flying overhead might miss it. Its edges have been smoothed by time, its towers cloaked in ivy. It juts out of the mountainside like it grew from the ground itself.

"It's perfect," I breathe.

Morgan nods, his breath fogging in the cold air as the sun meets the horizon. The sky bruises blood-red, the light turning golden as it washes over the castle.

"Holy shit." Lance appears on my other side, his face entranced. I inch closer to Morgan, and Lance glances down at me, a line creasing his forehead.

"Gigi, about before—"

"Let's go." I set off walking again before he can say something else. I don't want to be teased right now, not even in a friendly way. This morning's laughter is still ringing in my ears.

It takes another forty minutes for us to reach the castle entrance. As the daylight bleeds away and stars come out overhead, Morgan and a few of the others flick on flashlights to illuminate the path. I have one too, buried deep in my pack, but I don't bother fishing it out.

I'd rather stay close to Morgan's elbow and borrow his pool of light.

I glance up at the castle every few feet, committing each new angle to memory. Away from the trees, gorse and heather blanket the mountainside. In the distance, I can make out the white splotches of sheep, and a few bigger shapes that could be ponies or mountain goats. But as the light fades and the castle becomes a shadow, I stop gazing around and watch my feet instead.

"It was a hunting lodge until a few decades ago."

I nudge Morgan. "I know."

I sound unbearably smug, even to my own ears, but Morgan just nudges me back.

"You should write that paper," he says, out of nowhere.

"I already said I will."

"Good."

The castle entrance is as understated as the rest of the keep. There's no showy drawbridge or portcullis—just a large wooden door, notched with age, with iron patterns curling around the edges.

Morgan waits for the others to catch up, stroking a palm over the wood. The trio arrive first, Asher trying to catch my eye, then Annabelle and Thabo soon after. Professor Walsh is last, red-faced from the climb, his breath shuddering in and out of his chest.

"Come on then," he snaps between gasps. "Get on with it, Morgan."

Morgan turns back to the door, his lips pressed in a firm line, and slams the great iron knocker against the wood. The sound booms through the stone walls, echoing through the castle. A bird bursts out of a nearby tree, flapping and cawing into the sky.

We stand in awkward silence, our boots scraping over the loose shards of rock. I count to twenty heartbeats, but nothing happens.

I lick my lips. "Maybe we—"

Footsteps echo inside, approaching the door. I slam my mouth shut and step back, tucking behind Morgan's shoulder.

A deadbolt scrapes to the side, then the door groans as it swings on its hinges.

"Party from Llewellyn College? Yes. Come in, come in."

An elderly man stands to the side, and we file past him one by one. As soon as I step over the threshold, the scent of smoke and cold stone fills my nose.

A torch flickers in a bracket, lighting up a small lobby. I beam at the sight—actual firelight!—and my enthusiasm is only slightly dampened when I see the smoke alarm fixed to a ceiling beam and the fire extinguisher tucked in one corner.

Practicalities, Gigi. You'll be thankful for the running water.

There's a thick, handwoven rug on the flagstones, its wine-red tones muted by dusty footprints. Squat leather sofas circle a shadowy fireplace, and pages from historical manuscripts line the walls in glass cases.

"Huddle up."

Professor Walsh gathers us around the sofas, taking pride of place in front of the fireplace. He glares at us one by one, like we're rowdy teenagers and not serious students he brought here by choice. When his eyes reach me, I drop my gaze to my knees, picking at a hole in my leggings.

"You'll split into two groups for your special study. Topics must be approved by Morgan or I by tomorrow evening." I tune Professor Walsh out as he repeats everything he already told us by email. Honestly, why bother writing it down in the first place? It's not until he says my name that my head snaps up again.

"Good of you to join us," he says nastily. "Gigi, you'll work with Mr Lockford and Mr Penderly."

Melissa sucks in a breath on the other sofa. I glance over at her, my heart thudding in my chest. Professor Walsh doesn't notice the ripples of discontent, droning on to list off the other group.

"I will supervise Miss Penderly's group." The professor's gaze lingers on Melissa's flushed face. A bead of sweat slides down the back of my neck. "Morgan, you take the others."

Melissa pushes to her feet, already arguing, but the castle caretaker steps in front of the fireplace. He begins to talk, heedless of whether anyone's listening, and after a moment the chatter dies down.

Sleeping arrangements. Facilities. Rules for guests.

Nothing a fool couldn't put together.

Except for one detail—two of the rooms have sets of twin beds. The caretaker holds up a wrinkled piece of paper, his hand trembling so much I'm surprised he can read it.

"Lance Lockford and Asher Penderly in one room." He clears his throat and licks his lips. "Melissa Penderly and Gigi Russell in the other."

Melissa throws up her hands, arguing even louder, and I blink as Annabelle shoots to her feet and asks to share with me instead. I've never had someone try to argue their way into my presence. I beam up at Annabelle, practically glowing.

It's no good. And, crucially, it doesn't matter.

Group assignments and roommates. These are paltry concerns.

I'm here. I'm in Cariadon Castle.

The home of legends and lore.

* * *

I've never set foot in a castle before. Sure, I've been to historical buildings, but everything in the US is still so new. Even the oldest historical sites in America are babies compared to the crumbling ruins of Europe.

If I were the sort of person to believe in ghosts, this place would make the ideal pilgrimage. All these old castles are stuffed full with stories of murder and betrayal; of tragic deaths and political treachery. I know full well that ghosts do not exist, but a secret thrill runs down my spine when the shutters bang and the wind sounds like moaning.

"Spooky," I murmur to myself, adjusting the lens on my camera. I refocus on the tapestry hung in the great hall, running the length of the feasting table. The rough threads weave together to form intricate pictures - detailed accounts of famous battles in the area.

I snap a photo of a knight falling backwards off his horse, an arrow protruding from his helmet.

Grim? Well, that's history for you.

"Do you recognize the battle?" a voice calls across the hall. I glance over my shoulder to find Morgan warming his back by the vast fireplace. His hands are buried in his pockets, his shoulders relaxed, and I tamp down my knee-jerk reaction to snap at him.

Not everyone wants to make fun of me. I need to remember that.

"No." I speak quietly—it seems wrong, somehow, to raise my voice in these hallowed halls—but my words carry easily across the empty room. "But I could guess."

"Go on, then." Morgan's voice is warm. Faintly amused. I chew on my lip, considering.

"Well, they built the castle to defend against the Welsh. And most of the battles in this area were between the Welsh princes and the English invaders."

Morgan nods, strolling forward. I turn all the way to face him, my camera forgotten in my hands.

"Keep going." His low voice is like a caress.

"So it would be fair to assume the same of this battle. Another struggle for the rule of the land."

Morgan stops at my shoulder, eyes roving across the tapestry. He has that same hungry, yearning look that I feel plastered over my own face sometimes. He loves this stuff. Lives and breathes it. Without thinking, I sway an inch closer to my kindred spirit.

"Notice anything strange?" Morgan points to a figure tucked away in the tapestry's background. I follow his finger, squinting, then suck in a surprised breath.

"It's a story. Not a real battle at all."

Behind the chaos of knights and peasants, fighting with bows and swords, a figure crouches beside an apple tree. His face looks the same as any other man in the tapestry, and the rest of him takes a second to sink in. Small horns curl out of his hair, and his bare chest turns to a furred torso and fawn's legs. A lion's tail whips around behind him, swiping at the apples in the tree.

There are others, once you've noticed him. A two-headed dog under an upturned cart. Folded wings on the back of a knight's horse. I stare at the tapestry with fresh eyes, picking out all the hidden monsters.

"You already knew." I keep my eyes fixed on a peasant with a forked tongue snaking out of his mouth. "Why did you make me guess? Are you making fun of me?"

I feel rather than see Morgan whip around to face me. His

grip lands on my arm, gentle but firm.

"No! Of course not. I thought you'd enjoy the game."

I nod, holding my camera up to my eyes and snapping a photo of the reptilian man.

"I did. I'm just checking."

Morgan shifts. His hand is still on my arm.

"I'd never make fun of you, Gigi."

I lower the camera and shoot him a smile. Morgan smiles back, relieved.

"Sorry." I bend to pick up my camera case and pack it gently away. "I guess I'm not used to people being nice. But I mean, you're our tutor. Even if you hated me, it would be pretty unprofessional to show it."

"I don't hate you," Morgan says immediately. "Far from it. You're smart and sweet and interesting. In fact—and this is top secret—you're my favorite student, Gigi."

They're lovely words, but my heart sinks in my chest when I hear them. Morgan has always been kind to me; is always happy to help with research back at college. He even saved notes for me when I caught the flu last semester and couldn't make it to class.

No one else did that. No one else even noticed I was gone.

I know Morgan's a great tutor and we're lucky to have him. I know all that. But a ridiculous part of me doesn't want to be his student.

I want to be more.

* * *

I toss my camera case onto my bed and hear a crinkle of paper. Digging a folded note out from under the case, I wrinkle my

41

nose as I smooth out the creases.

Who leaves paper notes these days? The castle has WiFi.

And while I'm all for getting in the spirit of things, if you wanted to be historically accurate, you'd tie the note to a pigeon.

It's messy. Blotched with ink. I don't recognize the scratchy handwriting, but it's from someone with poor penmanship, apparently. I have to squint to make out the words, and when I do, I drop the note like I've been burned.

Meet me in the stables.

That's all. Nothing else. No reassurances, on the one hand, and no blackmail threats or ransom demands on the other. I wrack my brain, but there is no good reason for someone to lure me to a secondary location. And I'd be a fool to go—never mind that the note is unsigned. The detective at my future murder trial would roll their eyes.

I run through everyone on this trip. All the people who bear grudges against me.

Melissa. Lance. Professor Walsh.

Meet any of them in the stables? No, thank you. Call me melodramatic, but I plan to die of old age.

Screwing the note up into a ball, I toss it towards the waste paper basket. It bounces off the rim and onto the flagstones, shifting in the breeze creeping under the door.

I bite the inside of my cheek and ignore the scrape of paper over stone, tucking my camera away in a bedside drawer and digging my pajamas out of my backpack.

The note shifts again, skittering onto the rug. I sigh and drop my pajamas.

Just a glimpse. I just want a tiny peek at whoever left me that note. I won't actually go and meet them; I'll hide and see who it is.

I bundle myself into a dark sweater before good sense can kick in.

It's not that long after dinner, but the corridors are empty. Torchlight gutters on the stone walls, casting weird shadows over the oil paintings dotted everywhere. Anemic faces with empty eyes stare down at me as I hurry past.

The stables. Or ex-stables, anyway. There are no horses in Cariadon Castle these days—poor Mr Evans would never get a moment's rest—but the structure is still in place and used for storage.

I cross a small courtyard to reach the stable door. The cobblestones are slick with rain and uneven, and I lose all hopes of stealth. I pick my way across, cursing and muttering when I almost twist my ankle two times.

"You came!"

My eyes take a minute to adjust to the gloom. I am officially a terrible sleuth. I stand in the doorway, blinking and flustered, as my mystery note-leaver gets a good look at me.

"Who is it?" I glare into the darkness. I make out a jumble of shapes—stacked furniture and wooden crates, cloaked in shadows. Finally, a flash of movement draws my eye to the third stall in the stables.

"It's Asher. Sorry. I figured you knew."

He walks out of the gloom, palms raised.

"You didn't sign your note. How the hell would I know?"

"Well, I mean. Do you get many notes?" I turn to leave, but he lunges forward and grabs my elbow. "That came out wrong. I didn't mean it like that." Asher sighs and drops my arm. "I'm saying all the wrong things with you, Gigi. This is a shit show."

A spot of rain lands on my cheek, and I glance up. The night

43

sky is dark, the stars blocked by black clouds, and the next drop of rain comes down harder. I shuffle back through the doorway just as thunder rumbles overhead and rain begins to drum on the cobblestones.

"I'm sheltering from the weather," I tell Asher. "Not putting up with your shit."

He nods and steps back to give me more room. I wrap my arms around my waist and try to think of warm thoughts.

Open fires. A summer day at the beach. Curling up under the bed covers.

A shiver wracks through me, chattering my teeth, and I hug myself tighter. So much for the power of suggestion.

"Here." Asher moves to stand next to me, his arm lined up against mine. It's not an intimate touch—not an attempt at a hug. Just two strangers sharing space, like in any crowded elevator.

His warmth seeps through my sweater, and I inch closer. Damn it.

"Don't you want to know why I asked you to meet?"

I shake my head.

"Huh. Not even a little curious?"

I gnaw on my bottom lip, trying to figure out how to ask him without letting him win.

"It's okay, I'll just tell you. I wanted to talk to you alone. To apologize for before."

I roll my eyes, though he can't see me. That's it? He drags me out here to apologize, and now it's all supposed to be okay?

"It's a pretty weak apology if you have to do it where no one can hear." I press closer, despite myself. Asher's heat burns through his clothes, and the wind gusts sheets of rain inside the stables, soaking the front of our clothes.

"That's not why I brought you out here."

"Then why?"

Asher shrugs, his shoulder nudging mine.

"You know. History. Medieval stables. I thought it was cool."

For the first time since I got here, I look around us properly. Now that my eyes are used to the gloom, I can see the structure of each stall. The thick, weathered wood; the hooks and pegs for bridles and other riding tack. Even now, decades since horses last lived here, the air holds the sweet, nutty smell of straw.

"It is cool," I mumble. "You got that bit right."

Asher nudges me. "Got to count my wins, huh?"

We stayed on a ranch once for a family vacation. Most of the horses were huge and snorting: all bulging muscles and rolling eyes. But there was this one stallion the color of sand, who was so calm the others all relaxed in his presence. He used to amble over when I visited his paddock, and lean his whole body against the fence. He nosed at my pockets for carrots and mints, and close his eyes when I combed through his mane.

Sometimes, Asher reminds me of that stallion.

I watch the rain bouncing off the cobblestones for a while. Then, I tell him: "Don't laugh at me again."

Asher nods hard, his hair tickling my cheek. I fight the urge to reach up and comb it.

"I never meant to laugh at you at all, Gigi. But I swear it won't happen again."

We stand there in silence, listening to the thunder roll over the mountains. And when the rain eases off long enough to hurry back across the courtyard, Asher doesn't leave me behind. He grips my elbow, steadying me over the cobblestones, and positions himself to block most of the wind.

I guess he's not terrible, really. Even if his handwriting sucks.

Chapter 4

I take a scalding sip of coffee from my thermos and place it back on the wooden desk with a thud. The library is hushed, silent except for the crackling turn of pages and the two groups' breathing. Occasionally, someone mutters to their group, their low voices echoing off the stone walls.

I push my glasses up the bridge of my nose and pore over the map laid out on the desk. It's a copy, of course—they'd hardly allow a random American student to get her greasy fingers all over real historical artifacts—but the original map hangs on the wall in a glass case, and I can compare the two with a glance.

Hand-drawn, in green and blue inks. Mountains and rivers; cities and towns. There are monsters, too—mermaids off the coast; a two-headed man in the hills. I chew on the end of my pen, staring at the map with fierce concentration.

"Have you tried Google Maps?"

Asher's voice is loud, bouncing through the library. Lance glowers over from a nearby table, and Melissa's head snaps around from where she's sat with her group.

I sigh and look up at the man towering over my chair. He grins down, blue eyes crinkling and hopeful, and for a moment a crack opens in my chest. Then I remember him laughing at me in the forest clearing, and it seals straight back up again.

"Can I help you with something, Asher?"

It's his turn to sigh. "We're supposed to work as a group."

I frown at the extensive notes I've compiled on my laptop screen. I don't understand. This is how group work has progressed for me on every previous occasion.

"I'll share my findings with you and Lance. By the end of the working day, I promise." I give him what I hope is an encouraging smile. "You don't have to worry, Asher. I'll get it all done."

Something clouds Asher's expression, but then his face shifts and he's back to normal.

"That's not what I meant, Gigi." He pulls out the chair next to me. "May I?"

Social convention dictates that I nod. He drops into the seat and scoots it closer. Reaching over me, Asher spins the laptop to scan over my notes, and I'm hit with a wave of his scent.

He smells... fresh. Minty. Like the pine forest.

I shift on my chair.

Asher keeps talking, murmuring things about my notes and our group project. I half listen, mostly focused on the square line of his jaw, and the way he gnaws on his bottom lip between sentences. Asher looks like he'd be more at home in a wet suit than a library, his muscled torso stretched over a surfboard as his strong arms cut through the waves.

"Do you surf?"

Asher stalls mid-sentence as I cut him off.

"Uh. Yes. Back home. How did you...?"

I shrug, pleased that the version of Asher in my head matches up with reality.

"Just guessing."

48

He picks up the thread of his argument again, eyes flicking to me then back to the laptop screen. I smile at him, trying to seem encouraging. Yes, he hurt my feelings in the clearing. He shouldn't have grinned at Melissa's barb.

But he's trying, and he's so pretty up close. I'm rarely in proximity with people, and it turns out Asher is as much a work of art as the map on the wall.

"Maybe we could focus on this section more, use the local records..."

Asher trails off as I press the tip of my finger into the dimple in his cheek. He stills, staring straight at the laptop screen, like I might spook if he turns to face me.

Across the room, Thabo clears his throat and murmurs to his group. The library is quiet except for the crinkle of turning pages and the tap of laptop keys. I trace my fingertip from Asher's dimple down to the corner of his mouth.

"Gigi," Asher murmurs, barely moving his lips. Lance looks up just as I steal a glance at his table, and his eyes fix on my fingertip. Asher's cheek flushes pink beneath my feather-light touch, and a rush of power floods through my veins.

Lance glares at me, eyes stormy.

I don't know what gets into me. I wink.

Lance's chair squeals on the tiles as he shoves it back, abandoning his laptop and bag as he strides out of the library. The slam of the door echoes through the room, and three faces turn to Asher and I.

I tap a note onto my laptop, supremely innocent, as Asher drums on the arm of his chair.

"I should check on him," he says at last, pushing to his feet. I nod without looking up, chewing on the end of my pen.

So much drama on day one. These boys are such emotional

beings.

* * *

My study partners fail to return for the next several hours. I don't mind—honestly, I'd get this done faster alone—but after a while, concern gnaws at my insides.

Did I cross a line, winking at Lance like that? Taunting him with my flirtation with Asher?

No. I slam my pen down and push back my chair. Lance teases people all the time, including me. Especially me. He should certainly be able to take a joke.

I try the lobby first with its squashy armchairs, then the kitchens, then the guys' bedroom. They're not there, but I linger for a moment in the doorway anyway, trying to guess whose bed is whose.

Sheets tucked tight with military corners and a battered copy of a sci-fi novel on the bedside table: Lance. It's common knowledge that Lance spent the last few years before college in foster homes. That beat-up paperback with its escaping pages; the compulsive neatness reflected in those sheets—if I were the betting type, I'd put money on that bed belonging to Lance.

Besides, the opposite bed is sloppily made with a sweatshirt strewn over the covers. The sweatshirt has a cartoon shark with a plastic bag dangling from its tooth, and a protect the oceans slogan arching above in bubble writing.

Asher. He is famous for his questionable choices in sweat-shirts.

I never find the lovely Asher, but I do stumble across Lance in the castle armory. Back when Cariadon Castle was a defensive keep, the armory would have rung out with the clash of steel and the hiss of steam. Now, it's a museum display, with glass cases lit up from the inside.

Crossbows. Longbows. Swords and maces. In one corner, a full suit of armor, with a very off-putting dent in the chest plate.

Lance stands with his arms crossed, staring at a glass case of arrowheads.

"Should I alert the guidance counselor?" I call from the doorway. Once upon a time, the armory was open to the elements, but the museum is closed off like any room. I shuffle inside as Lance turns around, the door clicking shut behind me.

Lance jerks his head at the suit of armor. "People have had worse days."

I grin and wander closer to the case. The dent was only one of the knight's problems. There are gashes in the metal all over the thigh and arm plates.

"I'm sorry I winked at you."

Lance huffs. "I don't care about that."

"You did storm out."

"I exited the room. Calmly."

It's my turn to scoff. "You stormed out in a mood like I'd insulted your mom."

The military corners on Lance's bed sheets flash across my mind, and I bite my tongue, but Lance doesn't flinch. I guess he's not oversensitive about everything—just me flirting with Asher.

When he comes to stand at my elbow, I frown at the suit of the armor like it's the most fascinating thing I've ever seen.

"Don't mess Asher around," Lance tells me softly. "This isn't a joke to him."

It's not a joke to me either, but I'm hardly going to confide my feelings to Lance Lockford. Instead, I draw myself up to my full height and try to judge whether I'd fit in the suit. I'm not far off, height-wise, but about three of me would fit in the torso.

"Gigi."

I sigh and look at Lance.

"Do you think I'd fit in there?"

It's the wrong thing to say. His expression shutters, then he's closed off and cold again.

"We should get back to work," he mutters. "Let's get this group thing over with."

So they can get away from me again. That's what he means. I nod, gazing at the helmet, avoiding his eye until he finally turns and leaves.

It's surprisingly small, compared to the body. I wonder if it would snag my hair.

* * *

"Gigi."

The low voice finally filters through the names, dates and theories swirling round my head. I blink and look up from my laptop, the library dim except for a single lamp.

Morgan stands in the doorway, leaning a shoulder against the jamb. From his relaxed posture, and the faint amusement tugging at his mouth, I assume he has been trying to get my attention for a while.

"Yes?"

Morgan chuckles and pushes off the door frame, strolling into the room. He glances around, hungry eyes roving over the bookcases lining the walls; the maps and portraits hung on the cold stone.

"You missed dinner." Morgan's eyes don't leave the bookcases, so I take a moment to absorb every detail of his appearance. His shoulders are sturdy under his dove gray shirt—solid enough that you can see the structure of his bones through the fabric. His collar is open at the throat again, and my eyes snag on his Adam's apple.

Is that supposed to be a sexual feature? I want to lick it. I want to press my ear against the column of his throat and listen to his voice reverberate.

One of Morgan's hands leaves its pocket and rakes through his dark hair. It sticks up in a messy trail where he's touched it, but I don't want to pat it down. I want to twist my fingers through the neat parts instead, to make him really rumpled.

"Well?"

Morgan smirks at me like he knows what I've been thinking. I cross my legs and squeeze my thighs together.

"Well what?"

"Why did you miss dinner?"

Oh. That.

"I was busy."

It's a half-truth. I was making excellent progress with my research, yes, and I didn't want to lose the flow. But I also still felt tired from the journey, and the thought of eating under Melissa and Lance's glares made me sag in my chair.

Not my bravest moment, perhaps. But I'm not afraid of them—let me be clear.

I simply believe in choosing my battles. And after my scouting trip to the kitchens, where I glimpsed soggy boiled vegetables and dry cuts of beef, dinner hardly seemed worth the trouble.

"Liar."

I open my mouth to argue, but Morgan tosses something onto the copy of the map spread out in front of me. When I peel open the cloth napkins, I find a crusty bread roll, a hunk of cheese, and six ripe cherry tomatoes.

My stomach rumbles, the sound deafening in the silent library. Morgan quirks an eyebrow, sliding into the chair opposite me.

"Thanks." I tear off a chunk of bread, scattering crumbs over my papers.

"No problem. Just don't make it a habit, Gigi."

I can't help myself. A snicker escapes my lips as I pop the bread on my tongue.

"What?"

I chew carefully, eyeing Morgan's frown.

"Nothing," I say after I swallow. "I just like it when you're stern."

Morgan's eyes heat, even as his mouth twists.

"I'm a staff member, Gigi. Your tutor." His fingers drum on the wooden table. "You can't say things like that."

I roll a cherry tomato between my finger and thumb.

"I can think them, though."

Morgan hums, the low sound sinful. It tickles all the way down my spine.

"That's true. No one can police your thoughts. It's the one place in the world that's truly yours."

I like that. I like it so much, I press my laptop shut. Without the sickly blue light, the library seems warmer. More golden.

I lean forward, crossing my ankles under my chair.

"Shall I tell you what happens in my thoughts?"

Morgan's eyes flick to the open door, then back to me. He doesn't say yes, but he doesn't say no either, his lips pressed in a firm line. His jaw is clenched so tight, I can see a muscle twitch.

"In my thoughts, you close the library door and lock it. Seal out the world. Then you stride over here, lift me up, and spread me out on the table like that map."

"All right." Morgan holds up a palm, face strained. "Why are you telling me this, Gigi?"

I lean back in my chair.

"Because everyone thinks I'm cold inside. Dead, like some kind of machine. Just because I think differently, see the world differently, doesn't mean I'm not an animal at heart. I'm flesh and blood and urges—the same as everyone else."

I wind myself up as I speak, clenching a napkin in one fist until my knuckles go white. Melissa's snide comments, the way Lance glares at me with Asher—I hadn't realized it got to me so badly. But here I am, hiding away in the library and skipping dinner so I won't have to face them. So I won't have to see myself as others see me.

I force my hand to relax, dropping the napkin on the wood. I don't meet Morgan's eye as I brush the crumbs from my fingers and slide my laptop and notebook into my bag. The rest, I can deal with tomorrow—including Morgan's gift. I leave the creased napkins and pieces of food in a heap, scraping back my chair.

I'm not hungry anymore. Emptiness claws at my stomach, but queasiness clenches my throat.

"Gigi."

I ignore Morgan as I pack up. Why did I say those things to him? Why did I touch Asher like that this morning? They

55

probably both think I'm insane. *Freaky Gigi.* I wish I could take it all back, scrub away the touch of my fingertip and swallow those words down, but I am a practical girl. I know it's too late.

"Gigi. Look at me."

The zipper on my bag catches, and I wrench at it, face hot. It moves less than an inch before jamming again, and I screw my eyes shut, pulse thudding in my ears.

Fine. I'll carry it in my arms. It's just a zipper. Just a bag.

I repeat that mantra in my head as I open my eyes and scoop up my things.

"Just a zipper. Just a bag," I mumble under my breath as I round the table. Morgan's hand shoots out and grips my wrist.

"Are you all right?"

My face twists as I meet his eyes.

"It's just a zipper."

Morgan frowns but nods. His thumb rubs over my pulse point like it has a mind of its own.

"I can fix that for you."

I shrug, my things lurching in my arms. A pencil clatters to the stone and I ignore it, ears ringing.

"It's just a bag."

"Gigi—"

I pull free, his grip loosening easily. Morgan watches me walk to the library doorway, his gaze hot on the back of my neck.

They're just words. A day, a week, a year from now, they won't matter at all. Even as humiliation churns my gut, I know in my soul that Morgan won't tell anyone what I said. And maybe Asher will let me play off my touch as nothing, too.

I can say he had a crumb on his lip. Leftover from toast at

breakfast.

This is salvageable. I lost my mind for a few moments today, the heady spell of this isolated castle muddling my head. But I know why I'm here, and I know what is real.

I know who I am. I'm Freaky Gigi.

* * *

When I shoulder the door to my bedroom open, I nearly drop the bag in my arms. Melissa Penderly lies on my bed, her platinum blonde hair spread out on my pillow and her ankle crossed over one knee. Her foot bobs to some imaginary tune, clad in a fluffy blue sock.

Her eyes slide to me as I freeze in the doorway, her smile sly. "Hi there, roomie."

I take a deep breath and imagine a steel rod running the length of my spine. Kicking the door shut behind me, I step into the room.

"You're on my bed."

Melissa glances down at the quilted bedspread and the carved mahogany frame.

"Oh. Would you look at that?"

I stomp across the dusty rug and dump my broken bag on the foot of the mattress.

"Get off my bed."

"Get off my brother."

I pinch the bridge of my nose.

"They're hardly the same thing."

Melissa swings her legs onto the floor and sashays across the flagstones to her side of the room. A winter chill seeps through the stone floors and the glass window, but a small fire crackles in the hearth. I close my eyes for a moment and let the pop and sizzle soothe my racing heart.

"Don't touch him again."

"It was a toast crumb," I tell her, testing out the lie. Melissa scoffs, and I dismiss it for future excuses. She rants on, her voice hissing with fury, as I scan my bedspread and side table.

Nothing obviously out of order. Of course, in an ideal world, I could change the whole bed and start from scratch, but something tells me that Professor Walsh would not tolerate that. I have to trust that Melissa has not done anything truly vile.

One glance at her angry face, two spots of color glowing high on her cheeks, does not fill me with confidence. I flip the top corner of the bedspread back, checking the sheets.

"Are you even fucking listening to me?"

"Not really," I murmur, running my palm over the fabric. It's rough, clearly worn, but free from suspicious lumps or residue.

"Hey." A hand clamps down on my wrist, squeezing much harder than Morgan. I watch Melissa's fingertips turn white with detached interest.

"Yes?"

"Leave him alone. I'm serious, Gigi. Asher's not like you. He… feels things strongly."

I cock my head, still frowning at her grip on my wrist. Of course, I have no frame of reference, but I've never considered my feelings weak. Sometimes my heart clenches so hard in my chest, I wonder if I'm having a heart attack.

Like now, for example. My face may be blank, but my stomach is sinking all the way to the icy floor.

"What does that have to do with me?" I ask, choosing my words carefully.

Melissa's grip pulses tighter, then she finally lets me go, shaking out her fingers. I watch the white imprint of her fingers on my wrist fade as the blood rushes back.

"Nothing. It's none of your fucking business. That's what I'm telling you."

I turn my head and force myself to meet her gaze.

"Perhaps you should call me Freaky Gigi. It might sink in better."

Melissa's lip curls, her hands twitching towards me like she wants to grab me again. I slide back a few inches, just in case. She paces after me, her feet silent on the rug.

"If that's what it takes. I'll do anything to keep Asher safe, Gigi. Anything."

I don't know what to make of that. I'm hardly a natural predator.

I settle for nodding, my eyes snagging on the wall over Melissa's shoulder. She lets out a sigh and finally walks away, padding back to her side of the room.

Whatever. It's not like there's anything between Asher and I, anyway. He probably found me touching him creepy, like his sister did.

I kick off my boots and crawl into bed fully dressed, tugging the covers up to my ears. As the fire crackles and Melissa hums along to some song, I count backwards from one thousand.

It doesn't help. The lump stays lodged in my throat.

* * *

Two days later, Asher corners me on the castle ramparts. We've come up here in groups, bundled up in thick coats and layers against the icy January wind. White flecks of snowflakes drift around us, catching on woolly hats and exposed locks of hair.

Every breath is heavy with the fresh scent of pine and earth. The trees surround the castle on all sides, some drawing level with the highest turrets. Their branches tickle at the stained glass windows and scrape tracks of moss from the stone walls.

"You're being weird."

I bite the inside of my cheek and ignore the man at my shoulder. Resting my notebook against the ramparts, I sketch the surrounding landscape.

"I'm afraid you'll have to be more specific."

A gloved hand curls around mine, stilling my pencil on the page. I risk a glance at Asher and note that his mouth is turned down.

No crinkly, smiling eyes today. No delectable dimple.

"You're avoiding me," he says, voice rough. I jerk my head around, looking for his sister, but Melissa is nowhere in sight. Annabelle and Thabo work nearby, their backs turned to us, and Morgan leans against the castle wall, his gaze heavy on Asher's hand on mine.

"I'm not avoiding anyone. I told you, I work better alone."

"Bullshit." Asher crowds closer, his warmth washing over me even through my layers. "That's bullshit, Gigi."

His hand still rests on mine, but he's not clenching me in his grip. Asher is gentle, careful with me. It makes my stomach swoop.

"I'm sorry I touched you like that," I blurt. "I shouldn't have done that. It was weird."

One corner of Asher's mouth tugs up.

"Maybe it was a little weird." My heart sinks at his words, but his thumb rubs the back of my hand. "I liked it though, Gigi. I hoped you would do it again."

I glance around again, mouth dry, but Melissa is still gone. Morgan's mouth twists when he meets my eyes, and he pushes upright, striding away. His boots echo against the stone, the wind tugging at his dark hair.

I try not to stare after him. Like he said, he's my tutor.

"Like this?"

I lift the hand not gripping my pencil and graze the corner of Asher's mouth with a gloved finger. A smile spreads over his face at my touch, liquid and golden, and only the warm weight of his hand keeps me from floating into the cloud bank.

"Yeah. Exactly like that."

I smile back at him, dizzied.

Asher doesn't glance around before he crowds me against the ramparts. He doesn't check who's looking, or take a deep breath to ease his guilty, pounding heart.

He's a much better person than me.

One arm cages me in on each side, but I don't feel trapped. Even when my notebook and pencil slide to the floor, I can't bring myself to care. I'll brush the dirt off. I'll smooth out the pages. This—the way Asher looks at me, his blue eyes sliding over my features like he wants to commit me to memory—this is worth it.

"Gigi," he murmurs, his breath warm on my cheeks. "I want to kiss you."

I swallow hard, wishing for one helpless moment that I'd been more diligent with my lip balm regime.

"Are you sure?"

Asher lets out a strangled laugh. "One hundred percent certain."

I nod, chewing that over. I'd rather not be someone's experiment, after all. Asher's eyes bounce between mine as I weigh up the risks, a small line creasing his forehead.

"All right," I rasp eventually. "Since you're certain."

Asher's face cracks into another smile, sunshine breaking through the clouds and bathing him in a golden glow. He leans down, craning his neck to reach me, and pauses with his lips barely touching mine.

"Thank you," he murmurs, his words humming through my skin. I can't wait any longer. I lunge up and snag his bottom lip between my teeth.

Asher groans, sealing our bodies together and kissing me, his mouth tender. His hands are gentle as they cup my jaw, his fingers twining in my hair, and I don't even mind that he's probably smearing my glasses. I cling to the front of his coat and kiss him back, hard, pouring every painful doubt I've felt over the last few days into his lips.

I've never done this with someone I know before. It's heady; a thousand times better.

When we finally break apart, Asher rests his forehead against mine. Our chests heave under our coats, and I'm relieved to see he's as affected by this as I am. His pupils are blown wide, nearly swallowing up his glacier-blue irises.

I nudge the tip of his nose with my own. It's cold. Probably numb. Our breath clouds mingle in the freezing air.

"That was nice."

Asher laughs, the sound like warm honey.

"Very nice."

I lick my lips. "Do you want to do it again?"

"Right now or in the future?"

I shrug, teeth starting to chatter. "Either. Both."

Asher traces the tip of his freezing nose over my flushed cheekbone and into my hair. He sucks in a deep breath, smelling me, and it's so primal that heat floods my core.

"Both sounds good." He nibbles on my earlobe, and I dart a glance around us. Thabo and Annabelle are long gone. Just like Morgan.

The thought of our stern tutor dampens the fire roaring in my chest. I flatten my palms on Asher's chest and push him back a step.

He frowns at me, concerned, until I bite my lip and smile. Then he grins and twirls my hair around his finger.

"Let me kiss you again later. Promise you will, Gigi."

I suck in a deep breath.

"Okay. I promise."

Chapter 5

I t takes two hours and forty-three minutes for everything to fall apart. We meet in the library in our groups after lunch, scheduled to work on our joint projects. Thabo winks at me when I walk through the doorway, Annabelle laughing at my flushed cheeks.

I don't mind it. It's a friendly kind of laugh.

I give them an awkward wave and edge around their table, ignoring the twin lasers boring into my back from Melissa's glare.

Guess she heard about the ramparts. News sure travels fast in this castle.

Asher and Morgan sit at my table, bent over my map. Asher is relaxed, his shoulders fluid as he stretches to read a town name. Morgan sits upright, his spine rigid, a pen clenched in one hand.

Lance isn't here yet. I offer up a small thanks to the hypothetical heavens, and slide into my chair between the two men.

The tension is so thick at this table that it practically crackles in the air. At least I can get my head on straight before Lance storms in here and tosses a lit match.

"Good lunch?"

An easy smile curls Asher's lips as I nod.

Morgan mutters something under his breath about me finally eating. Asher glances at our tutor, a frown creasing his brow, but I clear my throat before he says anything.

"There's a sunken city. Have you seen?" I tap a section of ocean off the map's inked coastline, blurting out the first thing that comes into my head. The spot I'm pointing at is partway between a sketch of a woman with a shark's tail, and a giant octopus wrapped around a wooden ship. "The locals say they can hear bells ringing under the waves at low tide."

"That's awesome."

Asher reaches down and grabs the edge of my chair, tugging me a few inches closer. I wobble, gripping the table for balance, and look up just as Asher rests his arm along the back of my chair.

Lance Lockford glares down at me, his shoulders so tense he's practically vibrating. I shuffle forward on my seat, leaning my elbows on the table so that Asher's arm isn't touching me anywhere.

It's too late. Lance slams his bag onto the floor and drops into the chair opposite me.

"Right. Let's get started." Morgan rubs his eyes, his voice exhausted. I consider offering him the coffee in my thermos, but I bite back the words before I cause a riot.

"Oh, Gigi's been working on this for weeks," Lance spits. He's not talking about the project.

"Easy, man," Asher says, pulling his arm off my chair and leaning forwards. They hold each other's gaze, sharing some unspoken communication.

I've never had that with someone. I'd like to try it someday. Without thinking, I glance at Morgan and find him already watching me. Wordlessly, I raise my eyebrows and nudge my thermos towards him by an inch.

Morgan looks down, shaking his head, but a secret smile tugs at his mouth.

Huh. It's easier than I thought it would be.

"Let's get this shit show over with," Lance grumbles, scooting his chair closer. Asher's arm settles back on the edge of my chair, and he glares at his friend across the table like he's daring him to say something.

God. These guys are so damn fraught. It almost makes me miss being back at campus, where I can go for stretches of days or even weeks without speaking to another human being. According to my research on several notable psychology websites, emails to my parents do not count as high-quality social interactions.

Right now, I almost miss those lonely, peaceful days. But not quite.

We pass the study session in tense quiet, only speaking to each other in clipped sentences. The weight of Melissa's gaze makes me itch, and before the first hour is up, the kernel of a headache forms behind my right eye.

"This is painful," I grumble, pulling my glasses off to rub my eye with the heel of my palm.

Lance levels me a look.

"Finally, we agree on something."

* * *

After two false starts, I finally gather my courage and knock on Annabelle's door. Through the thick, aged wood, I hear the clatter of something dropping to the floor.

66

"Just a second!"

I rock on my heels, rehearsing my invitation in my head. I only manage one full run-through before Annabelle throws the door open, her dark hair slipping out of its ponytail.

"Oh, Gigi. Hi!"

She looks surprised to see me, that much is certain, but I don't think it's a bad sort of surprise. She quickly rearranges her features into a smile.

"Hello."

Annabelle nods at me, encouraging. I take a deep breath and clasp my hands together.

"I'm going to take a walk around the castle. See some notable features. I was wondering if you wanted to come."

In the silent rehearsal in my head, I'd sounded a lot more eloquent. Less stilted and weird. But Annabelle's smile stretches wider, and she holds up a finger before turning back to her bedroom. I crane my neck over her shoulder, taking in the smaller, private room.

A bed, a chest of drawers, and a deep-set window with stained glass. No fireplace, though. She must be cold.

"We have spare blankets in our room," I offer as Annabelle steps back into the doorway, shrugging a chunky cardigan over her shoulders.

"I'm fine, Gigi. Thank you, though. You're like my guardian angel on this trip."

I like that. I swear I grow three inches as we spill out into the corridor. And when Annabelle slips her arm through mine, hooking her elbow, I have to slip my free hand into my pocket and pinch my thigh.

Yep. This is definitely happening.

We wind our way through the whistling corridors, stepping

carefully on the uneven flagstones. The caretaker, Mr Evans, gave us a whistle-stop tour when we first arrived, but we haven't had a chance yet to soak it all in.

The cool stone. The scent of the mountains drifting through the windows. The rugs and tapestries and carved mahogany furniture.

"Is it what you expected?" Annabelle asks as we pause in front of a huge stained glass window. The rich, colored shards make up the image of a tower, with a river winding away from its base. On the river, floating through the reeds, a medieval woman rests on a boat, eyes closed.

"Yes and no." I huff, searching for the right words and exasperated at my lack of communication skills. "I researched the castle before we came. So I saw photos and read descriptions. I knew which artifacts and rooms to expect; knew what the castle looks like from the valley."

"But?"

"But there's only so much you can glean from a photo. I didn't fully expect the cold, or the way the wind howls through the windows. And there's something else about the castle. It makes me—makes me feel..."

"Unsettled?"

I shoot Annabelle a grateful smile. "Yes. Unsettled."

It's not just Cariadon Castle—I've been like this since we set foot on the plane. Awkward, restless and stifled, like my skin is three sizes too small. But it's more acute here, in the echoing halls, under the flickering glow of torchlight.

I don't feel quite myself.

Annabelle shudders, tugging me closer as we walk.

"Don't tell me there are ghosts here, Gigi. I'm a wimp."

I laugh, the sound bouncing off the walls.

"No ghosts. Just lots of legends."

"Same difference," Annabelle mutters, and I hum.

"I won't tell you the one about the beheaded man who came back to life the next day, then."

"That's fucking grim."

I shrug, a smirk spreading over my face. "Hey, I didn't write it."

We round the corner of the corridor and my steps falter as we see who's coming our way. Asher strolls along the flagstones, his hands in his pockets and his blond hair bright against his forest-green sweater. He jerks his chin up when he sees us, a grin stretching his mouth, and I swear the entire castle must hear my heart thundering in my chest.

Annabelle pats the back of my hand where it rests in the crook of her elbow.

"Thanks for the walk, Gigi. Maybe we can finish it tomorrow?"

I nod, flushing pink as Annabelle shoots me a knowing smirk and turns back the way we came. Hands clenching my sleeves, I stand there like an idiot as Asher closes the last twenty feet between us.

"Hi," I manage when he stops in front of me.

Asher takes me in with hungry eyes. "I just knocked on your bedroom door."

I snort before I can help myself.

"Bet your sister loved that."

Asher rolls his eyes. "Melissa can be overprotective. It's a twin thing."

I glance around; the corridor is empty apart from us, our shadows entwined on the wall. The sight makes me bold, and I inch closer, lifting one hand to fiddle with the hem of Asher's sweater.

"Do you need protecting?" I watch a loose green thread slide over my thumbnail.

Asher tips my chin up.

"Let's hope so."

His mouth is hungry when it meets mine, his hands sliding into my hair. Asher clutches my face to his like I might slip through his fingers, even as I squeeze handfuls of his sweater in my fists and tug him against me. My glasses ride up my nose, and I make a mental note to dig my contact lenses out more often.

"I want you," I murmur between kisses. Asher groans into our kiss, and I feel it all the way to my toes. This is moving fast. Maybe I'm supposed to act harder to get, supposed to be more coy, but I don't understand those rules and right now I don't give a shit.

I want him. I want Asher Penderly so badly I can't see straight.

"Lance is in my room," Asher grinds out against my cheek. "Melissa is in yours."

I nod, head swimming as I cling to his broad shoulders. Are they this muscled from surfing, or from another sport? I vaguely recall that Asher and Lance are both on a sports team at college, but I never cared enough to take in the details.

Sports are not really my thing. Wrong sorts of legends.

"It would be wrong to ask Lance to leave…"

I float the idea without committing to it. Such a chicken.

Asher laughs, but it comes out bitter.

"Yeah. I'm afraid so."

I suck in a deep breath through my nose, forcing myself to concentrate. My pulse thunders in my wrists, my temples, my core. The second Asher touched me, I lit up like the torches hanging in iron brackets on the walls.

The corridor swims into focus over Asher's shoulder. It stretches along the western side of the castle, lit by pools of firelight. During the day, sunshine filters through the stained glass windows and paints the stones like gemstones. Now, at night, the windows are dark and the flagstones are gray.

Mid-way down the corridor, an alcove cuts into the thick stone wall. It holds a statue—a king from one of the local legends, pulling a sword from a stone. I grab Asher's hand and push past him, dragging him down the corridor.

"Here." I slide around the edge of the statue's plinth. The statue gazes on at the sword in his hand, unperturbed by our arrival. Asher glances up and down the corridor before squeezing in after me. His shoulders catch on the wall and the plinth, and it takes some contortion for him to join me at the back of the alcove.

There's a little more space here. Breathing room. The statue towers at my back, blocking us off from view, and when Asher steps in front of me, he's bathed in shadows.

"Gigi," he murmurs, sliding his palms over my hips and up the sides of my rib cage. "There's not room to do everything I want to do to you here."

I shrug, acting more casual than I feel. What I want to do is shriek at the ceiling at the feeling of Asher's hands on me. I want to slam him back against the alcove wall and suck my bruises into his throat.

"We'll make the most of it," I tell him instead. "And use the room another time."

My mouth slams shut as I realize what I've said—the assumption I've made out loud. Who says Asher wants to do this twice?

None of my past partners have before.

But he's nodding, leaning down to nose at my jaw.

"You're right." His tongue flicks out to tease the pulse point on my throat. I shiver, reaching out to anchor myself by his belt loops. "I'll just have to impress you here first."

I'm already impressed, but I don't tell him that. I don't want to discourage Asher from striving for greatness. Especially not when it means him crowding me against the statue's base and pressing the line of his hard cock against my hip.

I sigh and roll my torso, rubbing myself against him. Asher grunts and bends to pick me up, his arms scooping under my thighs.

"I can't think straight when you do that," he says, depositing me on the plinth. I spread my legs and he steps between them, my pussy in line with his stomach.

"We're at the wrong heights."

Asher rubs a soothing palm down my thigh.

"No, we're not. This will do just fine."

I don't know what he means by that—unless he has a truly monstrous cock—but I let him shuffle me to the edge of the plinth. I lift my hips as he tugs my leggings down, taking my underwear with them, and he pulls the fabric all the way to the tops of my boots.

"What are you doing?"

I'm not afraid, just confused. This is not how my sexual experiences have gone. And if Asher goes too off-script, there is a higher risk that I won't know what I'm doing and I'll disappoint.

Then he might not want a second encounter. That would be... upsetting.

"Has anyone ever done this for you, Gigi?"

Asher runs his palms up and down my bare thighs. He's obviously talking about something else, something I should have guessed by now.

I grit my teeth and force the words out.

"I'm not sure. I don't understand what you mean."

Realization dawns on Asher's face, and he gives a small nod before leaning forwards. He captures my lips with his, kissing me gently before sucking my bottom lip into his mouth and nipping it. I gasp, straining forwards, desperate for him to touch my bare core. My pussy is molten against the cool stone.

Asher pulls away, resting his forehead against mine as he traces a finger up the inside of my thigh. I hold my breath as he nears my core, but he draws a quick circle and swoops back down to my knee. He ignores my growl, doing it again and again as he talks.

"I want to kiss you here. Make you come with my mouth. Would you like that, Gigi?"

"Obviously," I huff. "I'm not an idiot."

Asher chuckles and nudges my knees wider. He grasps an ass cheek in each hand and tugs me forward until I'm balanced right on the edge of the plinth. If he let me go and stepped away, I'd topple onto the flagstones, my leggings tangled in my boots.

I run the cost-benefit analysis of this risk and decide to let him do what he wants. Asher does not seem like the type to let a girl fall on her face, and I desperately want to feel his mouth on me. The second he said those words, I'd never wanted anything more.

"Trust me," Asher murmurs, as though he can read the tension in my body. I take a deep breath and try to relax.

The press of his lips to the inside of my knee has me jolting upright all the same. Asher kisses and nibbles and licks his way from my knee to the very top of my thigh, then switches to my other leg and does the same. I plunge my hands into his hair and grip handfuls of the soft strands, tugging sharply when he dances away from my core a third time.

"Are you lost?" I hiss, frustration sharpening my words.

Asher chuckles, and without warning, seals his mouth to my core.

The first broad stroke of his tongue through my folds makes my eyes roll back in my head. This—the silky feeling of his lips and tongue on me, the way he eats at me like he's a starving man—this has been a viable sexual activity this whole time? I mentally curse my feeble earlier partners, moving to grip Asher's shoulders and swaying backwards as my hips twitch from pleasure.

Fuck. He makes me—fuck. Every tiny sound and motion from him—hell, even his fresh, manly scent—it all ratchets me higher and higher until my thoughts evaporate into smoke. For the first time in my life, I'm not thinking. I'm not a rational, intellectual person.

I'm a gasping, heaving animal, and I whimper like one. My boots scrabble against the plinth for purchase, but Asher presses my thighs apart and keeps me helpless. I roll my hips towards his face and he sucks my clit into his mouth, sliding a finger into my pussy at the same time. He crooks his finger, rubbing at a spot on my inner walls, and I lose it.

I've never come like this before.

I shout out—I can't help it—and my thigh muscles spasm under his bent shoulders. Asher grips me tight, holds me through it, still lapping at my clit, and white spots appear in my vision, pleasure thrumming through me until the tension finally snaps.

I slump against the statue man's legs, pulse thudding in my ears. I open my mouth, but no words come out. He's ruined me.

Asher straightens up and smirks at my dazed expression, his eyes glittering. Holding my gaze, he slides a finger into his mouth and sucks it clean. I stare at his hollowed cheeks, wet and shining from my pussy, struck dumb.

It can be like this? What the hell.

* * *

Melissa surges up from her bed when I slip through the doorway. It's past midnight, but she's fully dressed, her hands balled into fists.

"Where were you?"

"Hello, Mom." I shut the door with a snap and turn to face the enraged harpy on the rug. "I've been out playing with friends."

Melissa scoffs and rolls her eyes. "You don't have friends."

I shrug, keeping my features blank despite the sharp throb of pain in my chest. It doesn't matter what Melissa Penderly thinks—I've made friends here: Annabelle, Morgan and Thabo. And I'm not sure whether what I just did with Asher was *friendly,* exactly, but I'm pretty sure he likes me, too.

"Are you going to ground me?" I ask mildly as I cross to my bed. "Take away my allowance?"

"Where have you been, Gigi?"

Goddamn it. What is her problem? I toss my sweater onto the bedspread and whirl to face her.

"I was with your brother. He went down on me in an alcove. Are you happy now? Do you need more details?"

Melissa visibly shudders, her face chalky white.

"I told you to stay away from Asher."

"And I told you it was none of your fucking business."

For a split second, Melissa frowns, confused.

"Uh… no, you didn't."

"I didn't?" Huh. "Well, I thought it."

We're off track, but I don't care. I'm done with this conversation. I'm tired of being Freaky Gigi, of being warned away from Asher Penderly like I'm some kind of psycho and he's in danger.

I'm different, yes. I expect that's true. But I'm not fucking evil. And if she thinks I'd willingly harm one of the few people who treats me normally, she's the one who's insane.

I sigh, pinching the bridge of my nose and gathering my thoughts. Then I fold my glasses and place them on the bedside cabinet before I speak, so I don't have to watch Melissa's expression.

"I like your brother. I won't hurt him. And I won't be scared away. So whatever twin-bit you've got planned, whatever you're going to threaten me with, you should save your breath." I glare at the blurry bedspread. "For as long as he wants me, Asher is mine."

There's a long pause, then the scrape of a wooden drawer. Melissa digs through her clothes, tossing what I assume are pajamas onto her bed.

"Whatever, Gigi," she mutters, so quiet it's on the edge of hearing.

I hunt down my own pajamas, lips pressed tight together. The happy bubble in my chest from my time with Asher is long gone, deflated by his sister. I slide between the sheets ten minutes later, teeth brushed and face scrubbed, and roll over to face the wall.

The firelight dances over the stone, and I watch it, vision fuzzy.

I won't be scared away. If only I could convince myself, too.

* * *

The flagstones are icy beneath my bare feet. The warmth and weight of the bedspread slides away, and I list to one side as I stand. The threadbare rug muffles my footsteps as I cross the room, the air chilled now the fire has died out. My roommate snuffles in her sleep, her face mashed into her pillow.

The iron door handle creaks as I turn it to one side. The heavy wooden door groans on its hinges as it swings open, and I step out into the corridor.

Where am I? I don't... I don't understand.

I'm not really here.

My feet lead the way, carrying me along the flagstones and taking two left turns. I strain to do something, to make sense of this, but my thoughts are heavy and muffled. I frown, my forehead creasing under my bangs, my steady footsteps leading me to a wooden door.

Recognition tickles at the back of my brain—I reach for it, but it evaporates like steam. The wooden door is scratchy under my palm as I push it open, gritting my teeth against the weight. It's heavy, but smooth on its hinges, swinging open to another dark, silent room.

My footsteps carry me to the center of the floor. There is another rug beneath my numb toes.

Two sets of breathing come from two different beds, pushed against opposite walls. My body turns of its own accord, leading me directly to the farthest bedside.

The bedspread is rumpled. I grasp it in one fist and fold it back

77

from the sleeping form beneath it. A tiny voice shouts in the back of my head, even as I climb onto the mattress and slide in next to the warm, muscled body.

The man stirs, mumbling something in his sleep and rolling over to meet me. Strong arms wind around my waist, gathering me to a hard chest and ridged abdomen. I press closer, sighing, my palms sliding over hot, bare skin.

"What—what are you—Gigi?"

The voice is rough from sleep and angry now, jerking me back by the shoulders. I reach for him again, eyes glassy and unfocused.

"What the fuck... Asher! What's wrong with her?"

Footsteps thud over the stone, then gentle hands turn me onto my back. I whimper and reach for the man beside me again, but those hands catch mine and hold them to my chest.

"I don't know. I think... I think she's sleepwalking."

The new man's voice is strained.

"Should we wake her?"

"No!" He clears his throat. "No. I've heard that could hurt her."

The body beside me gusts out a sigh, tickling my bangs against my face.

"Well she can't fucking stay here, can she?"

There is silence for a moment.

"Swap beds with me."

The man in the bed grumbles but sits up, starts to clamber over me, but I wrench my hands free and slide my palms up his neck. He stills, shuddering with tension, and I rub my thumbs along his jaw.

"Asher," he whispers.

The second man says nothing. A feather-light touch skates over my cheekbone and into my hair.

"Stay with her, then," he says at last. "Until she wakes up. But Lance, don't—don't touch her."

The man above me is icy when he speaks.

"I'm going to pretend you didn't say that. What the fuck kind of monster do you think I am?"

There's a grunt, then footsteps walk away. Clothes whisper against skin as one man dresses on the other side of the room, while the other lowers back to the mattress. I reach for his warmth, rolling towards him, but he nudges me onto my back again.

"Oh, no you don't. Asher. Where are you going?"

"Out. I can't watch this."

"Asher, wait—"

The door thuds closed. There's no sound except for our breathing.

"Now you've fucking done it," the man mutters, settling back down beside me. He won't let me turn, but I inch closer until I'm pressed up against his side.

A happy sigh escapes my lips, and I feel the man tense.

"Come on, Gigi," he mutters. "Wake up. We need to have a fucking word."

I stare unseeing at the ceiling, warmth spreading through me from the body next to mine. There's a thought, needling at the back of my brain, but I can't latch on to it. There's only the soft mattress, the scent of wood smoke, and the delicious heat of bare skin.

My eyelashes flutter closed, and darkness drags me under.

Chapter 6

I wake up in the wrong bed. These sheets are darker, and they smell masculine. Like wood smoke and citrus and something else. I sit up, the bedspread pooling around my waist, and I squint around the strange room. My heart thunders in my chest as a thought occurs to me, but when I pat my torso and my legs, my pajamas are still on.

Sleepwalking. I press a palm to my chest, trying to soothe my rapid heartbeat. I've been sleepwalking again.

Whoever usually sleeps in this bed, they're long gone. The room is silent except for the crackle of a small fire in the grate. I can't make out details, but my eyes are good enough to recognise the hue of pre-dawn light shining through the stained windows.

Time to get out of here.

I swing my feet out onto the flagstones, wincing at the cold. My nipples pebble beneath my pajama top, and I wrap one arm over my chest. There will be enough questions already. No need to humiliate myself further.

The corridors are mercifully empty as I tiptoe back to my bedroom, tracing my fingertips along the stone walls. It takes me several wrong turns, squinting into the gloom, before I finally recognize our bedroom door.

Melissa's snores drift over from the corner of the room. I let myself in as quietly as I humanly can, not in the mood for more interrogations. Unlike last night, it would be entirely reasonable for her to freak out about this latest development.

I woke up in a strange bed. I don't know whose it was, or whether they slept there with me.

Fuck. I hope it was Asher's.

There's no way I could go back to sleep now, so I dig out fresh clothes and a towel. I wander down the corridor, glasses perched on my nose, to take a long, scalding shower.

While I'm in there, I briefly consider drowning myself, but my heart's not in it. Drowned girls don't get to sleep with Asher Penderly. And there's a chance, at least, that it was his bed I woke in, and I haven't screwed this all up.

That tenuous hope melts away the moment I step into the breakfast hall.

Asher and Lance sit at a long table, jaws clenched as they eat in stony silence. Melissa is not here yet, mercifully, but Morgan sits opposite them, papers spread over the wood.

I could leave. Pack a backpack and take to the woods, like some feral wild child. Create my own legend in the Welsh legends—a blonde Bigfoot with bangs.

Asher glances up and gives me a strained smile. I pick my way between the tables.

"Um." I hover by the empty seat between Lance and Asher before rounding the table and drawing out a chair next to Morgan. I drop into it and place my palms flat on the wood, taking a deep breath.

I should have grabbed coffee on the way over here. This conversation is already going to suck. Goddamn it.

"Sleep well?" Morgan asks before I can say anything. I frown at him, suspicion curling through my gut.

"Sort—sort of. I, um. I need to ask something."

He smiles at me, encouraging. I glance over at Asher and Lance, and find them both glaring at their plates.

Well. That rules one of them out, I suppose. Ignoring Morgan, I spin on my chair and cut to the chase.

"Who did I sleep with last night?"

Morgan chokes on a mouthful of coffee. He splutters, scrabbling for a napkin as I fix my gaze on Lance and Asher in turn. They both look exhausted, with dark shadows under their eyes, and Lance's tawny hair is rumpled. Asher turns to his friend, expression pinched.

"You didn't stay with her?"

Lance scoffs, tearing a piece off his toast. "You can't fucking talk."

Well. There's my answer. Why my subconscious took me to Lance Lockford's bed, God only knows. But it's done, and there's nothing I can do to take it back—no matter how much Asher's tired eyes break my heart.

I nod once, pushing my chair back.

"Right. Okay, then. My apologies for the inconvenience, Lance." I clear my throat. "I'm sorry, Asher."

Morgan catches my wrist before I can leave, his grip firm.

"Someone explain this to me. Now."

His words are quiet, but an undercurrent of fury runs through them. I don't know why Morgan out of everyone is the most pissed off, and it throws me off balance.

I frown down at the papers spread over the table, latching onto place names and dates. I read them each three times, committing them to memory. Anything to escape this conversation.

Distantly, I hear Asher sigh.

"Gigi sleepwalks, it seems."

I chew on the inside of my cheek, tears blurring my eyes. Caerphilly. St. David's. Anglesey. They're wonderful names. Loaded with meaning. So many stories in each.

"And?" Morgan prompts, his thumb rubbing circles onto my wrist. I dart a glance at the clean white crescent of his thumbnail, then fix back on the papers.

"And she climbed into bed with me," Lance finishes with a huff. "Not that it's any of your fucking business."

Morgan ignores him, ducking his head to murmur in my ear. "Did they hurt you, Gigi?"

I jerk my head from side to side, a tear splattering onto the paper.

"No," I croak. "I just wondered where I was."

Asher curses and thumps Lance on the arm.

"I'm sorry," Asher says, his voice low and urgent, and I blink up at him, eyes still watering.

"You're not mad?"

Morgan stills, then places my wrist carefully on the table. Asher arranges his face into a smile.

"No. I'm not mad."

He doesn't look happy either, not really, but I suppose human emotion is a wild and wonderful spectrum. I nod at him, chewing on my lip, and barely cringe when Lance surges to his feet. I expect him to storm out, to slam the door and pronounce to everyone how freaky I really am.

Instead, less than a minute later, a mug of hot coffee lands in front of me with a thud. Lance twists the handle to face me, then squeezes my shoulder before walking back to his chair.

"Drink up, Gigi." He throws himself down in his seat. "Lord

knows you had a long night."

* * *

Five hours later, I leave Asher and Lance bent over our books in the library and slip out into the castle hallway. The library is on the top floor, elevating the books away from the damp soil, and the wind whistles through the stained glass windows as I wander along the rug. The dark lines of tree branches whip and wave, and I shiver on their behalf.

Tucking my chin into my sweater, I wind my arms around my middle and stroll to the second study.

Cariadon Castle boasts an endless warren of rooms and halls. Despite its modest size—from the outside, at least—there are enough twisting corridors and silent rooms that you could get lost for hours.

In so much space, it's no surprise that Professor Walsh has set up a makeshift office three doors down from the library. Why miss an opportunity to summon and dismiss people at will?

Morgan never showed up to our session after lunch, which probably means he's doing Professor Walsh's dirty work. I've seen it before: the professor heaping deadlines and assignments onto Morgan's shoulders, then taking credit for his grad student's efforts.

He's a troll. If there were justice in the world, Professor Walsh would be the assistant and Morgan would be in charge.

But this is the real world, where crusty, powerful old men win over handsome young assistants all the time. So when I knock on the study door and push it open, I smile wide at Professor Walsh.

"Hi, Professor." He grunts at me, barely glancing up from his makeshift desk. "Could I borrow Morgan for a moment, please?"

Morgan smiles at me from his spot by the bookshelf, a thick leather-bound tome in one hand. He slides the book onto the shelf, his shirt sleeves rolled to the elbow, as sunshine filters through the stained glass window and paints him purple and green.

Professor Walsh slides a look at Morgan.

"What do you want him for?"

Ah. I fiddle with the hem of my sweater.

"It's about that paper. The call for submissions." I know he won't like that—and sure enough, his eyes narrow. I pick at a loose thread on my sweater, stilling my fingers when the professor drags his gaze down my body to my hands.

Morgan drops a book on the desk with a slam.

"How can I help, Gigi?" he cuts in, and I shift on my feet. He sounds annoyed.

"I, uh. I was going to ask you to supervise. To read over my outline; workshop my draft. That kind of thing."

It's a big thing to ask, I know that, but it was Morgan who insisted I submit in the first place. He's surely my best bet for support, and if I really want to do this, I'll need all the help I can get. It's the first paper like this I've written, and I'll be competing with postgraduates and seasoned professors.

Morgan frowns and opens his mouth, but Professor Walsh speaks first.

"Why Morgan? Why not ask me?"

Because you're a prick.

"I thought you'd be too busy, sir." My words are right, but my tone is all wrong. He hears the distaste in my voice, and his lip curls.

"I am the head of the History department, Gigi."

"Yes, sir."

"Mine is the utmost opinion."

"… Yes, sir."

It takes all the social practice I've had since this trip began, but I school my features into a blank mask. Professor Walsh leans back in his chair, the wood creaking, stroking a finger over his lower lip. He used to be handsome. Still is, I suppose. You can tell from the cut of his cheekbones; from the broad chest stretching his waistcoat.

Too bad about his shitty personality.

"I'll do it," he clips out, even though I never asked him to. "But don't waste my time. Come to me when you have something worth reading, and not a moment before."

I flounder, searching for the combination of words that will save me from the hole I just dug. Professor Walsh is literally the last man in this castle I want to spend time with, and that includes the caretaker, Mr Evans, who smells of mildew.

"Thank you, sir," I say finally, drawing a blank. I guess Professor Walsh is supervising my paper.

Morgan gives me a rueful look when I turn to leave. Maybe someone better-versed in social interactions would have seen this coming. I shrug, face still blank, my shoulders barely moving half an inch, then let myself back out to the quiet corridor.

Damn it. That did not go to plan.

* * *

"Go fish."

Thabo blows out a breath, shaking his head. He plucks at the cards in his hand, spreading them out evenly. Annabelle takes her turn, asking for kings, and I glance around the reception room.

It's small. Cozy. A relic of the castle's hunting lodge days. Squashy armchairs cluster around a giant hearth with a set of antlers fixed to the wall above the grate. I wrinkled my nose when I spotted them; the notion of trophy hunting is not one I admire.

Threadbare rugs overlap on the flagstones, and the windows are high and cut deep in the walls. It's cool, down here in the base of the castle. We're in the belly of the beast.

"Go fish."

We play another round, chatting and only half concentrating. It's strange being here. Surreal. Like we're in a pocket out of time. I know it's just the surroundings—the isolation, the harsh beauty of the castle—but I'm glad I'm not the only one who's been knocked off-kilter. Melissa almost smiled at me earlier over dinner, before huffing and rolling her eyes at my dumbstruck expression.

The heavy wooden door swings open, and the rest of our traveling group files in. Despite being indoors, Lance, Asher and Melissa are all dressed in bulky hiking jackets. Asher makes a beeline straight for me, dropping onto the arm of my sofa, his hand gripping the back of my chair. Lance and Melissa take another sofa, chatting in soft voices, and Morgan strolls to the fireplace to run a finger along the tip of an antler.

Professor Walsh pauses in the doorway, running his eyes over each of us in turn. Finally, he grunts and leaves without saying goodnight, and a collective sigh fills the room.

"Thought he'd never go," Asher murmurs into the top of my

head, his lips pressing a kiss into my hair.

Melissa narrows her eyes at me from her sofa but doesn't say anything, turning back to Lance. They're relaxed together—far more relaxed than either of them has ever been with me. Melissa kicks off her boots and settles her feet in Lance's lap, his hands resting on them automatically.

Jealousy spikes low in my gut. I close my eyes and breathe through my nose.

When I open them, Lance has turned his head to the side, and the firelight picks out copper strands of his hair. I gnaw on my lip, soaking in every detail of his straight nose, the severe set of his jaw.

"What are you playing?" Asher asks, jolting me back to the present. The playing cards rest forgotten in my lap.

"Um." I swallow down the guilty lump in my throat. "A very simple card game."

"Helpful," Lance mutters, apparently listening after all. I stick my tongue out at him and he snorts. "Come on." He moves Melissa's feet from his lap and slides down onto the rug. "Let's all play something together."

"Poker?" Thabo suggests hopefully.

Lance produces a dusty bottle from the depths of his jacket and winks.

"Strip poker."

I'm not opposed to recreational nudity, but practicality leads me to choose a spot by the hearth. I lower myself to sit cross-legged beside Morgan's feet, glancing up to give him a smile.

"Will you play?"

Morgan sucks in a sharp breath and shakes his head. The fire casts deep shadows over one side of his face.

"I can't, Gigi. Tutor, remember?"

My mouth twists.

"Worth a shot," I mutter at the rug, quiet enough that only Morgan can hear. He chuckles, his fingers dancing out to play in my hair before he strides away across the flagstones.

"Have a good night," he calls, pausing in the doorway. "Try not to desecrate the castle."

The others laugh and wave goodnight to Morgan, but I stare after him, chewing my lip.

I don't like it when he goes away, back to Professor Walsh and his tyranny. He belongs here, with us.

With me.

"Ever played?"

Asher folds himself onto the floor beside me. He places an emerald green bottle between us—the same kind as Lance's.

"No. Where did you get those?"

Asher grins. "We paid off that crabby inn lady to let us raid her stash."

I prod the neck of the bottle, making it wobble on the uneven flagstones. Asher swipes it and turns the lid with a crackle, then swigs a mouthful of the clear liquid.

"Good?" I ask, doubtful. I've only ever drunk wine with my parents. There's a whole wonderland of alcohol out there to try, I'm sure, but I've never had anyone to drink with before. And many films and novels assure me that drinking alone is a path to ruin.

"Try for yourself."

I grip the bottle and tip my head back, taking a big mouthful. It stings my tongue, the fumes making my eyes water, but I pinch my nose and force myself to swallow.

"That's awful!"

Lance laughs at my spluttering, the firelight dancing in his

89

eyes where he's sat across the rug. Even Melissa's mouth curls up a fraction.

"Why on earth does anyone drink this?"

I'm deadly serious. That was like swigging paint stripper. Lance shrugs, his head tilting to one side, but Asher leans to murmur in my ear.

"So they can be brave." The tip of his finger runs down my arm.

Interesting. I knock the bottle back again.

* * *

I walk into the corridor wall, stifling my laughter in my sleeve. Melissa weaves along beside me, giggling at something her brother just said. It's late—God knows how late. Midnight has come and gone and now we're in those otherworldly morning hours when time doesn't feel real.

Usually, if I'm awake at this hour, it's due to a bout of insomnia. I'll pace around my bedroom or do stretches on my yoga mat or look up my favorite historical figures on Wikipedia.

It's never because I haven't tried sleeping yet. Because I'm having fun.

Lance wanders ahead of us, his sweater on back-to-front. He and Asher handle their drink better than Melissa and I, presumably because of their body mass, but they're both bright-eyed and grinning. For Lance, that's a personality transplant.

"We have to be quiet on this stretch," I announce too loud. "That's Morgan's bedroom."

We pass the door in question, and I trace my fingertips over the wood. A big part of me wants to turn that door handle and let myself in; to jump on Morgan's bed and see how he looks without his glasses.

I don't. I'm not that tipsy. But I hold my breath as we walk past, straining to hear any sounds inside.

"Keep up, Gigi." Lance calls down the length of the corridor, his arms crossed over his broad chest. I'd think he was still pissed at me, but a smirk tugs at his mouth. Melissa catches up and leans into him, an arm looped around his waist.

A hand slides into mine, tangling our fingers together, distracting me from the surge of jealousy in my gut.

"Where's the professor sleeping?" Asher asks.

I shudder. "Probably hanging from a beam in the attic."

Asher tosses his head back and laughs, the sound rich and golden, and triumph flares in my chest. I beam at him, and break into a jog as he pulls me along to catch up to the others.

I'm doing it. A late night party. Hanging out with *friends.* It's not so hard.

"Race to the room," Melissa announces as we clatter to a halt. She points at me, eyes narrowed but playful. "Jockey contest."

"I don't understand," I start to say, but Melissa circles around us and hops onto Asher's back. She grips his shoulders, her ankles crossing in front of his waist, and raises her eyebrows at me.

I look at Lance. He nods, face suddenly sour.

"We don't have to," I mumble as I step closer. Lance shrugs, and my heart sinks.

"She won't shut up until we play along," is all he says, then I'm winding my arms around his neck and being hoisted into the air.

My glasses slip down my nose, and I nudge them back into place. Lance is solid beneath me, his large hands gripping my thighs, and when I take a breath, it smells like his shampoo.

"Um." I lean down, my lips grazing the shell of his ear. "Your sweater is on backwards."

Lance huffs a laugh, then Asher takes off, and we thunder down the hall in pursuit. I hang on for dear life, the alcohol sloshing in my stomach, trying my best not to notice the feel of Lance's warm, toned body between my thighs. But my hands have a mind of their own, sliding back and forth on his broad shoulders.

"That was rigged."

Lance sounds strained when we enter the bedroom behind the others. He snatches his hands off my thighs like I've burned him, and I slide down onto the floor. For a second, the room teeters, tilting to one side, then a warm hand steadies my elbow.

"Easy."

Lance frowns down at me, his jaw clenched. I don't know why he's suddenly grumpy again, but I'd give anything to coax that grin back. I pluck at the front of his backwards sweater.

"Thank you, steed."

He catches my hand and holds it.

"Any time."

His words are friendly, but he's still frowning. And that crease in his forehead deepens as Melissa's voice rings through the room.

"Falling for Gigi's charms, too, Lockford?"

Lance drops my hand and steps back, his eyes sliding to Asher. Silence stretches between us, and I fiddle with my sleeve.

"I am pretty charming," I mumble when I can't bear it any more. Asher softens, his shoulders dropping an inch, and gives me a smile.

"Hell yeah. Ridiculously charming." He herds me towards my bed until the back of my legs hit the frame. His blue eyes dance as he cups my face, smoothing his thumbs over my cheekbones. "Did you have a good night?"

I nod, lips parting. Asher's hair skims his shoulder as he tilts his head.

"Thoughts on drinking?"

"An excellent life decision. I highly recommend it."

Asher grins and presses his mouth to mine.

"Save your final judgement until the morning," he murmurs against my lips. "Put a glass of water and an aspirin on your bedside table."

"Okay," I whisper, stifling a moan as Asher nips at my bottom lip.

A throat clears across the room. My cheeks flame as Asher winks and pulls away.

The door clicks shut behind the guys, and I steel myself before turning to Melissa. Her earlier playfulness is gone; her eyes are cold, her lips pressed tight.

"I won't warn you again, Gigi. If you hurt Asher, I'll make you sorry."

Chapter 7

Cariadon Castle has worn many identities over its hundreds of years. There's the battle worn keep, yes, designed and built to keep attackers at bay. But then there's the hunting lodge; the nobleman's summer home; the secret base for plotting against the English crown. In the nineteenth century, a famous astronomer stayed here for a winter to map out the stars.

And at some point in the parade of legendary visitors, a theater troupe passed through.

"God, I hope this isn't real fur."

Annabelle holds up a cape, her nose wrinkling. I know for a fact that it *is* real fur—they clearly did not have polyester when these costumes were made—but I decide to keep that insight to myself. For a theater troupe to use it, it wouldn't be valuable anyway. It was probably once an unlucky street cat.

"Smelly, aren't they?" I say instead. We found the enormous trunk of costumes in one of the castle's storage rooms. When we levered it open, a gust of mildew-laced air filled the room and sent the dust motes spinning.

"Stinking." Despite her grimace, Annabelle spins the cape and settles it over her shoulders. She looks regal, like the snooty oil portraits lining the castle corridors, especially when she waves imperiously. "Peasant? Fetch my wine."

I snort. "Can't, sorry. I've sworn off alcohol, my liege."

Turns out the giddy, floating feeling that comes with drinking is not worth the pounding headache and churning stomach the next day. I gulped down the glass of water Asher told me to prepare like it was the elixir of life, and I still felt like roadkill.

We chat as we rummage through the trunk, and I mentally congratulate myself with every social cue I pick up. Perhaps there's something to the old adage after all, and practice does make perfect.

Annabelle graciously never accuses me of hiding, even when voices pass outside in the corridor and I press myself against the wall out of view. I'm not scared of Melissa Penderly, not really, but my energy for fraught social interactions is running dangerously low.

Better to hide away and play dress up. These clothes are history in our hands.

"Oh, wow."

Annabelle whistles at the dress I lift out of the trunk. It's silver, the material woven to look like chain mail, falling to the floor in a shimmering cascade.

"Huh."

I've never bothered much with my appearance, but this dress makes me wish I tried harder to tame my hair this morning.

"Try it on," Annabelle urges. I lick my lips. I've never done this, not even as a child.

"All right." My throat is weirdly dry. "Watch the door."

The castle temperature ranges from chilly to sub-arctic depending on which room you're in, and we're far from a fireplace here. I tear my sweater and long-sleeved t-shirt off, tossing them onto the dusty flagstones, and pull the dress on over my bra and leggings.

"Which way… what the…"

Annabelle spins the dress around my shoulders so it's facing the right direction. She buttons me in with quick fingers, a grin spreading over her face.

Stepping back, she looks me up and down.

"Fucking hell," she says at last. "Those boys don't stand a chance, Gigi."

I flush and pretend not to know what she's talking about, plucking at the fabric over my stomach. It's scratchy and stale, hugging close to my skin. The storage room door scrapes open behind us and I jerk, nearly tripping over the skirts.

"Dinner is… oh."

Morgan stands in the doorway, one hand clenched around the doorknob. He gazes at me with an intensity that makes goosebumps erupt along my skin, his gray eyes sliding slowly down the length of my dress.

Annabelle coughs, stifling a laugh, and swings the cape off her shoulders. She bundles the material and drops it in the trunk, winking at me as she turns away.

"I just remembered I need to ask Thabo something. Excuse me, Morgan."

She slips past our tutor, turned to stone in the doorway, her footsteps echoing away down the corridor. I shift my weight, heat spreading up my neck when I realize I've been caught playing dress up by a graduate student.

"We were just…" I stall, clearing my throat, but I can't think of a mature excuse. My shoulders sag. "We were just messing around."

Morgan breathes in sharply and nods, stepping into the room. The door creaks shut behind him.

"They're theatre costumes," I ramble. Morgan's eyes flick to the trunk, then back to me. "Pretty old, I think. I don't know which play, but maybe something by Shakespeare—"

I break off as Morgan lifts a lock of hair off my shoulder and winds it around the top knuckle of one finger.

"It suits you." He sounds almost bitter about it. Resigned.

I force a nervous laugh. "Can't wear it to class, though."

Morgan shrugs, running the pad of his thumb across the strands of my hair. They look golden next to the silver of the dress. I'm a creature of metallics. A knight in figure-hugging armor.

He's so close. The scent of ink and paper clings to him from his work in the library, along with the fresh mountain air. My heart thumps in my chest, squeezing into a hard knot as I rock onto my toes, drawn toward him.

Morgan drops my hair and steps back, the corner of his mouth tugging down.

"Better get changed, then. Dinner's served."

He turns to go, but I grab his sleeve. The material slides over the hard muscles of his arm.

"Gigi…" Morgan begins to say, but I cut him off. I don't want to hear it.

"I need help with the buttons. That's all."

Morgan glances at me, a tortured expression flickering over his face, but it smooths quickly into a calm mask.

"Of course."

The line of buttons are down the side of my rib cage, under one arm. I lift it and turn so that Morgan can reach, his fingers brushing my skin as he works his way down the fabric. He passes the dip of my waist, the swell of my hip—all the way down to the waistband of my leggings. My heart beats out a rhythm against my chest, so loud he must be able to hear it.

"There." Morgan's voice is rough. "Do you need anything else?"

"No. Thank you."

He strides out quickly, the door clicking shut behind him, and cold air floods close in his absence. I shiver, tugging the dress off my shoulders and stepping out of the skirts.

I fold the fabric carefully, smoothing out any creases, and place it back in the trunk. The lid thuds closed, and I suck in a shuddering breath.

These are dangerous games.

* * *

Professor Walsh is holding court when I tiptoe into the dining room. He claimed the seat at the head of the table on the first day, like it was some kind of throne, and he spends each meal giving impromptu lectures on Welsh history.

Normally, it would be my idea of perfect dinner entertainment, but whenever Professor Walsh's eyes land on me the hairs prickle on the back of my neck. That man does not like me. And I do not like him.

"Late, Gigi!" he calls, interrupting his flow. I grimace and wave, sliding into the chair next to Lance.

"Sorry, professor."

He grumbles something under his breath, but launches back into his lecture. Lance's knee knocks mine under the table, and I give him a faint smile. Across the table, Asher's eyes flick between us, his fork forgotten in his hand.

With the professor droning on in the background, I dig into the steaming plate in front of me. It's some kind of creamy tagliatelle, piled high with mushrooms and flecked with herbs, and I bend so eagerly over my food that my glasses fog. A moan escapes me at the first garlicky mouthful, and Professor Walsh pauses before starting up again.

Oops. I widen my eyes at Asher before shrugging, already scooping up my next forkful. His eyes crinkle with amusement as he leans back in his chair, watching me eat, his own plate abandoned.

I swallow. "You're not hungry?" I murmur.

He smirks, nudging the toe of my boot with his own. "Starving."

A heavy hand claps down on my shoulder, making me jump. I blink up at Professor Walsh, the steam clearing from my glasses.

"I read the proposal for your paper, Gigi." His voice rings through the dining room, and all the faces at the table turn to me.

"Gr-great! Thank you, professor. Maybe we could discuss—"

"It won't do. It's a lazy, overdone topic with a tired argument. It's childish, to be blunt."

Professor Walsh goes on, listing my flaws at length, projecting his voice like he's still lecturing the group. I shrink in my chair, humiliation staining my cheeks red. At the other end of the table, Morgan clenches his fork so tightly his knuckles turn white.

Finally, the professor pauses for breath and I cut in before he can go on.

"Thank you, sir. Lots to think about." I hate how wobbly my voice sounds.

He smirks and leans down, squeezing my shoulder hard as he mutters in my ear. His breath is warm on my cheek, and I grimace.

"Don't let Morgan's weakness for you go to your head. It has nothing to do with excellence. Indulge his special treatment of you and it will ruin both of your careers."

He turns away, and I force myself to breathe normally. Tears blur my eyes as I pick up my fork and attack my cooling pasta.

It tastes funny. My stomach flips, and I place the fork down carefully, wiping my mouth on my napkin.

I worked so hard on that proposal. I studied before breakfast; during lunch; after dinner. I used local records which hadn't been cracked open in decades.

Is he right? Am I kidding myself, getting carried away because my tutor said some nice things?

"Forget him," Lance mutters in my ear, his voice urgent. "He's a shitbag, Gigi."

I nod, scratching at a mark on the mahogany table.

He is. A powerful shitbag, in charge of the department I want to work in one day.

* * *

I don't speak for approximately seventeen hours.

I'm not trying to be weird or difficult. But there's a lump in my throat that won't go away, and it feels like my tongue is fused to the roof of my mouth. Professor Walsh's words echo through my brain, and it's all I can focus on.

Childish. Lazy. Overdone.

Even Melissa gets sick of my silence, huffing as she scrubs at her damp hair with a towel.

"Perk the fuck up, Gigi. You know Walsh is full of shit." I nod, sitting on my bed to cram my feet into my boots. "Since when do you care what people think?"

I cock my head to one side, considering her question. The answer comes, but I don't speak it aloud. *Since I found people who like me for me.*

It's probably too much to hope this new weirdness doesn't put them off.

Lance and Asher prove me wrong though, making my doubts seem bitter and ungrateful. They seal themselves to my side at breakfast and stay there all day, chatting brightly to fill the void of my conversation. Every now and then, they toss me a question, faces hopeful, but they don't get pissed off when I fail to answer.

After a couple of hours, Asher butchers a Welsh town name and I manage a smile.

He punches the air like a preening sportsman.

Our study sessions are productive despite my newfound muteness. Morgan joins us at our table, gaze watchful as I move through the fragile pages of an old manuscript. The paper is crumbly beneath my special gloves, and I turn them with infinite care. The pages scrape against each other, letting off the most delicious old-book scent, and as I breathe it in, it soothes my soul.

"You're a natural, Gigi," Morgan says quietly.

I bite my lip and smile down at the faded text. But the pages I combed through to write that proposal cross my mind, and my mouth turns down.

"Fucking Walsh," Lance mutters. Morgan hums in agreement. Asher reaches over the table and takes hold of my hand. He flips it over so it's palm-up, glove and all, and starts to massage my thumb.

My eyes flutter closed. It feels so damn good.

"Did you enjoy the research?" Asher asks, voice low. I nod. "Then it doesn't matter. Maybe it's a strong proposal, or maybe it needs work, but none of it was a waste."

I suck in a breath and look up, meeting their eyes one by one. My voice is hoarse when I finally speak.

"I worked really hard."

"Fuck yeah. You always do." Lance sounds proud. I don't know what to do with that. Morgan watches Asher's hand on mine, his expression unreadable.

I clear my throat. "What do I do now?"

Asher leans forward, his chair creaking.

"You prove he's got you all wrong."

They're being so nice, all three of them, and when I glance over at the other group's table, Annabelle smiles and gives me a quick wave. My hand tightens around Asher's, holding him there.

I turn to Lance, asking the question that's been gnawing at me for days.

"Do you still think I'm freaky?"

To my relief, he doesn't just blurt out an answer. He chews the inside of his cheek, his brown eyes thoughtful, and actually considers my question.

"Not freaky," he says eventually. "I think you're different." His knee nudges mine. "In the best way."

Asher's hand tenses, but I don't let go yet. I nod briskly and turn back to the table.

"Good. Because I have an announcement to make. I'm attracted to all three of you."

The conversation across the room splutters to a halt, then slowly starts up again. I ignore it, focusing on the three men around me, cataloguing their reactions.

It's a risky thing to say. I'm aware of that. But I'm not good at social cues at the best of times, and I'd prefer we all be straightforward with one another. This way, everyone is fully informed, and they can make their own decisions.

And if they're angry, at least they weren't lied to. I'm sure that would be worse.

Asher sighs and pulls his hand from mine. His mouth twists as he looks at me, picking up a pen to fiddle with.

Lance shifts in his chair but doesn't say anything. Morgan sighs and stands up.

"I can't have this conversation. Let me know if you need help with your project."

I watch him stride out of the room, past Annabelle's sympathetic face and Melissa's furious glare. She can say what she likes. I tried my best. But this is too messy for me to navigate.

"I'm going to grab a coffee," Lance mutters, his chair scraping over the flagstones. Asher follows without a word, and I'm left with our table of maps and books, sitting in silence again.

Fine. I wasn't in the mood to talk, anyway.

* * *

The dungeons are just as ghoulish as I'd hoped. Tucked away in the lowest part of the castle, they smell of moss and wet stone. There are no windows, and the only sound is the steady drip of water into a puddle.

I huddle on a stone bench in the dark, resting my chin on my knees and closing my eyes. Drawing in a long breath, I try to imagine how it felt to be imprisoned here hundreds of years ago. Would they have heard the sounds of the castle? The clang of steel in the small armory; the hubbub of the kitchens?

Or would the thick stone walls have muffled the sounds, and forced them to listen to a drip just like this?

I scanned the small room with the flashlight on my phone when I first entered. There's nothing—no iron shackles on the walls; no implements of torture. Just a cold, empty room cut into a mountainside.

I shiver, clutching my knees to my chest. My heart feels battered, sore with every thump, but I breathe through it and focus on my exercise. I came here to learn, after all. To experience history first hand. And the cold, creepy desolation of these dungeons is not something you can learn from a book.

The darkness is so complete, there's no difference when I open my eyes. I hold my hand up inches from my nose, but I can't even see the shape.

Fascinating.

Footsteps echo on the winding stairs, and I press my sleeve to my nose, stifling my breathing. The person moves slowly—these steps are lethal; all narrow, slippery and cut at different heights—and I press back against the damp wall.

The footsteps pause. "Gigi?" Lance calls.

I count my breaths until he walks away. Real prisoners would not have had visitors. They'd be stuck here, alone and forgotten.

My reenactment is doomed, though. The footsteps which approach twenty minutes later don't pause midway down the stairs. They come down every step, the tread lighter than Lance, until the soles of boots crunch on the gritty dirt floor. The beam of a flashlight shines in my face, and I screw my eyes shut as white spots float in my vision.

"That's not historically accurate," I grumble.

Morgan chuckles. "Sorry." The light disappears, his phone

tucked back in his pocket. His boots splash through the puddle as he strolls to the bench, then Morgan lowers himself next to me.

"You don't need to hide. There's nothing to be embarrassed about. You haven't done anything wrong."

"I know that," I snap, shuffling away on the bench. "This is research."

I don't want to feel his sweet warmth seeping into my side. It's like a cruel joke.

"You… took them by surprise. Give them some space to think it over. They're close; they might come around."

"And you?"

The ceiling drips into the puddle.

"I wish I could, Gigi. Like you wouldn't believe. But I can't talk about this anymore."

Embarrassment and anger flood through me in equal measure. My skin flushes hot and itchy, and I surge to my feet.

"Why come down here, then? You brought it up! Is it so much better to risk getting caught together in the dark? How would you explain *this*, Morgan?"

I pace back and forth as I rant, boots splashing on the puddled floor.

"We haven't—I haven't touched you. I'm your tutor, and I came to check on you."

He's annoyed too, his voice rising, and I'd second guess myself if I weren't so pissed off. But no—I'm not making this up in my head. I'm a grown woman, a consenting adult, and he wants me. He just told me as much.

Striding toward Morgan's voice, I reach out until my hand meets a broad chest.

"Tell me to stop." Morgan says nothing, and I grip his sweater

105

in my fist. I clamber onto his lap, clumsy in the pitch black, and when my knees settle on either side of his torso, I wrap my arms around his neck.

"How about now?" I'm breathing hard, dizzy with this tiny victory. He told me he wants me; he didn't tell me to stop. "Are you my tutor now?"

Two palms slide up my hips before gripping my waist and tipping me sideways. I tumble onto the stone bench, one boot stomping in a puddle and splashing icy dungeon water up my leg.

"Of course I'm still your fucking tutor." Morgan's voice is low, hushed in the still air. He bites out each word like he'd rather be tearing strips off me. "What we want doesn't matter. It's called *restraint*."

He leaves before I can respond, his boots loud on the stone steps. I straighten on the bench, shaking, then suck in a deep breath through my nose and hold it to the count of ten.

Gusting it out, I rest my forehead on my knees.

I deluded myself. I don't understand this situation at all.

Chapter 8

"And you're sure this is an appropriate apology gift?"

Annabelle pats my forearm, bare from my rolled sleeves, and leaves a floury hand print on my skin. I blow my bangs out of my eyes and work the rolling pin over the dough.

"Definitely. Everyone loves gingerbread."

Well, that can't be true. It's messy and laborious and since my third piece of raw dough, I've started to feel sick. I gnaw on my bottom lip, wondering whether Morgan will view my apology cookies as another metaphorical slap in the face.

"And you're certain—"

Annabelle cuts me off.

"Gigi. It will be fine. Even if the cookies suck, it's the thought that counts."

I sigh and nudge my glasses up my nose, no doubt leaving a smear of flour. The kitchens look like a wild animal rampaged through, what with the dirtied pots and pans stacked everywhere. While I'm sure there are efficient and clean ways of baking, this is a skill I have yet to master.

Annabelle seems to think that makes the gift even better. Apparently you must suffer for a proper apology.

She chuckles to herself as she collects sticky spoons in a

bowl.

"I can't believe you climbed in his lap."

I close my eyes against the memory, humiliation prickling over my skin.

"I can't believe I did any of it."

Annabelle hums. "It was pretty badass, actually."

I don't know what she means, but I hardly think my ego needs further inflation. Rather than dig for compliments, I use the cookie cutter we scrounged up from the kitchen drawers to cut out eight little men.

It's weird using flimsy bits of plastic in a kitchen that's hundreds of years old. The castle has been updated over the years, wired for electricity and plumbed for running water, but it still messes with my brain to see a microwave perched on top of the old iron range.

You can still taste the smoke in the air. It's embedded in the stone walls; stained right down to the mountainside. I suck in a deep breath and slide the baking sheet into the modern oven, my glasses fogging up.

"It's a shame about this." I straighten and tap my fingernail on the hob.

Annabelle snorts. "Would you rather bake them over an open flame?"

Yes, I think, even as reason reminds me that I struggled to switch the oven on.

"What's all this?"

Melissa leans in the doorway, her platinum hair smoothed back in two immaculate French braids. I swipe at the flour on my nose with my wrist.

"Apology baking. We'll be done soon if you want to use the kitchen."

Melissa smirks and steps down onto the flagstones. They're bigger here than in other rooms, and stained black from smoke.

"Offended someone else? You're a busy bee."

I shrug. No point arguing with the facts. I brace myself for another Melissa Penderly jab, but it doesn't come.

"I'm glad you told them, Gigi. I didn't think you would. They deserve to know."

I blink at my frosty roommate, but her mouth is curled in a faint smile. Wordlessly, I offer her the bowl with leftover scraps of gingerbread dough. She plucks a piece out, holding it between finger and thumb, then tips her head back and swallows it like a seabird.

"Not bad." She grins at me, and I feel myself smiling back. "Asher loves ginger."

Ah.

"These are for Morgan, actually."

Melissa raises her eyebrows but mercifully doesn't push. Instead, she leans back against the iron range, crossing her ankles and tilting her head. She chats with Annabelle as we clean up, talking about next semester's course schedule and the spring sports season, and I listen like I'm part of the conversation too.

"Chosen your classes yet, Gigi?" she tosses my way as I scrub the flour off the counter. I jerk, thumping my head on the spice rack.

"Yeah—no." I rub my forehead. "Not yet."

That's it; those are all the words we exchange, but it feels like an Olympic victory. After a while, Melissa wanders back out the doorway, and I wait for the cookies with Annabelle by my side and a faint smile tugging my lips.

* * *

I knock on Morgan's door for a third time, a sigh escaping my lips. I've checked everywhere—the library, Professor Walsh's 'office', the living spaces. Annabelle and Thabo just started a game of checkers in the library, while the Penderly twins and Lance are stretched out chatting on the leather sofas in the lobby.

Morgan is nowhere to be found.

I press the tip of one finger gently to a gingerbread torso. The plate cools in my hand, the cookies hardening from gooey deliciousness to regular, room-temperature gingerbread. Damn it.

"He's not here."

I snap my head to the side, wincing at the twinge in my neck. Professor Walsh stands ten feet away, hands thrust casually in his pockets. His chestnut hair is glossy in the torchlight, and he's taken off his usual tweed jacket, leaving him in a waistcoat and shirtsleeves. His broad chest tapers to a slim stomach, and evening stubble darkens his jaw.

I can see why he has such a fan club on campus. Only among the freshmen, though. It's humanly impossible to lust after Professor Walsh after spending too much time in his presence.

"Do you know where he is?"

Professor Walsh cocks his head to one side.

"Are you very interested in your tutor's whereabouts, Gigi?"

This is a trick question. I blow my bangs off my forehead to put off answering.

"I baked him cookies," I say at last, since the plate in my hand is fairly damning. "To thank him for his help this week."

"That's interesting." Professor Walsh strolls two steps closer.

"Because I heard a rumor. Do you know what the rumor was?"

I shake my head. His question is a poorly concealed trap, and I'm not an idiot.

"It was about you, Gigi. Declaring to the whole library that you have a crush on your tutor—not to mention two other boys." Professor Walsh tuts, shaking his head. "Highly unprofessional behavior."

A sick feeling curls through my stomach. That stupid announcement was nothing compared to crawling into Morgan's lap in the dungeon. I literally threw myself at the poor man. Could he have told Professor Walsh?

Perhaps. If I put him in a difficult enough position.

"You're right, professor," I hedge. "That's what these really are: apology cookies. I crossed a line, and it won't happen again."

Professor Walsh hums and steps closer—close enough to reach out and twirl the end of my hair around his finger. I tense, my body rigid, but he doesn't touch me anywhere else. Just twirls my hair, round and round, the firelight glinting off the strands.

"Morgan is a boy." His voice is hushed, conversational. "Barely older than those others you like. If you two are even suspected of inappropriate conduct, both of your careers will end before they've begun." Professor Walsh glances up, his eyes burning into mine. "They're not worth the risk, Gigi. If you want to throw your future away for a fuck, you come to me."

He drops my hair, takes hold of my plate, and strolls away, my cookies in hand. I gape at his back, bile crawling up my throat, as my mind whirs through what just happened.

There was no one else here. No one overheard. It's my word

against Professor Walsh, and he's head of the department.

There's nothing I can do. I clap a hand to my mouth and fight down a retch.

* * *

The final day in the castle passes in an awkward, stilted blur. I time my arrival at breakfast with precisely eight minutes to spare—enough time to grab and ingest food, but not enough for conversation.

Not that anyone is clamoring to talk to me. But I tell myself that's for the best.

The study sessions with Asher, Lance and Morgan are the worst. We sit around our shared table in the library, tapping away at our laptops in silence. Everything I've said and done over the last few days hangs between us like a dark cloud, and it's all I can do to tamp down my anxiety enough to make final notes on our project.

We'll hand it in this evening, then we're done. Finished with the project, this trip, and each other. Then it's back to campus and regular life.

Back to long nights alone in my room. To stretches of days and weeks where I barely speak to another person.

I try not to think about it. I focus on theories, dates and names.

As soon as the clock face shows the end of our afternoon session, I surge out of my chair and pack up my things. I toss my laptop, charger and notebook in my backpack, only slowing down to handle the castle's books and maps with care.

"I'll deal with those, Gigi," Morgan says, eyes fixed on his screen. Lance and Asher hum in agreement, rolling up the replica map between them. Neither of them look at me, their gazes flicking between the mess on the table and each other.

All right, then. I shoulder my backpack and walk away.

I dreamed of Cariadon Castle for so long. The trip is an annual event for the college's History department; they brag about it in the brochures. The day I got my offer letter, this was one of the first thoughts to cross my mind.

A chance to experience history. To touch, taste and smell; to step foot on the hollows that boots wore in the flagstones hundreds of years ago.

I'm not finished with this place yet.

The others gather in the lobby. Their laughter bounces down the corridor, under-laid by the scrape of logs as someone coaxes the fire to life in the hearth. Asher and Lance will join them soon; maybe even Morgan. They'll all play cards and chat, the conversation coming easily. I walk past the turn for the lobby and continue down the stone corridor.

My boots thud on the uneven steps, winding upwards in a spiral. The wind whistles down the stairwell, numbing my cheeks and snaking into the neckline of my coat. I trace my fingers along the icy stone as I climb, half to touch where thousands of hands have touched, and half for balance. It's a long climb, steep and unforgiving, and by the time I spill out onto the ramparts, my thighs burn and my chest heaves for air.

The wind pummels me from all sides, snatching my hair and dancing it around my head. I squint against the icy cold and the violence of the gale, the trees groaning as they bend under the onslaught. Dark clouds hang swollen overhead, and I tuck myself back against the castle walls.

It's incredible. Like the wrath of gods.

Local legends scroll through my mind: folk tales of giants

and magic and earthquakes. Thunderstorms which rend the earth; great floods which cleanse the land.

I can see where they got it from, now.

Plastered against the wall, I don't notice the first hailstones. The *plink* of them bouncing off the ramparts filters through my brain, and then there are so many of them, they're impossible to ignore. White lumps of ice the size of golf balls, raining down on the mountainside and bouncing as they land. One hits my cheek, stinging, and another lances my thigh. Bright light flashes through the evening gloom as lightning cracks the sky.

Thunder booms, vibrating the mountain.

"Holy shit."

The wind snatches Melissa's voice and throws it into the trees. She steps out of the stairwell and presses against the wall, sliding along until our shoulders meet. I risk a glance at her pixie-pretty face, with her rosy cheeks and tiny, upturned nose.

Melissa's mouth drops open as she watches the gathering storm, hailstones pounding on her coat.

"They used to think thunder was the sound of giants fighting." I shout into her ear. "And the valleys and craters were where the giants fell."

Melissa nods to show she heard, eyes fixed on the black clouds. When lightning strikes, the clouds are lit from within, temporarily lightened to grey.

"I don't blame them," she shouts back after a moment. "I like that version better than science."

I grin, nudging her, then turn back to the storm. It unleashes its fury on the castle; the rocks; the trees. Briefly, I feel sorry for the sheep and wild ponies we saw on the hike to the castle door, but more than anything I feel tiny.

Small, insignificant, and very much alive.

I don't know how long Melissa and I stay pressed shoulder-to-shoulder on the ramparts. Long enough for the wind to tangle our hair together and our faces to turn to ice. Hailstones beat against the castle walls, catching us on the legs and torso, and still we stay out there, witnesses to the storm.

We only go inside when I feel Melissa shiver so hard that it vibrates through my coat. Without a word, I nudge her along the wall and back into the stairwell.

"That was fucking insane," she says, breathless, as she leads the way down the steps. It's slow going: they're treacherous at the best of times, and hailstones have blown inside and made them more slippery. The balls of ice clatter down the steps in front of us as we catch them with our boots.

"Have you heard of pathetic fallacy?" I ask, hearing how awkward I sound even as my mouth forms the words.

"Yeah. That's when the weather in books represents the character's mood, right?"

"Yes."

Melissa snorts, but it's not an unkind sound. "Is the hailstorm your doing, Gigi?"

I grin at the back of Melissa's head. "I wish."

We descend a few more steps before I gather the courage to speak again.

"I'm more of a steady downpour right now. You know, wet but not wild."

Melissa chuckles, the sound bouncing around the narrow stairwell.

"I like it. I'm probably sunshine with scattered showers."

The light fades as we get further away from the ramparts,

until I'm blinking hard against the gloom. The last dozen steps, I have to navigate by feel, palm plastered against the wall.

"You made me feel like a few downpours earlier in the week," Melissa says when I finally stagger out into the corridor. The torches are lit on the walls, their buttery light flickering over the flagstones.

"Why?"

I don't understand. I tried my best to keep out of her way.

Melissa sighs, hooking her elbow through mine and steering us towards our room.

"You did nothing wrong. I know that now. I was just worried about Asher. Lance too, I guess, but Asher especially. He's so gentle, and he likes you so much. I could tell you were interested in the others as well, but I didn't think you'd tell him."

I wrinkle my nose. "That wouldn't be fair."

Melissa squeezes my arm. "See, you get it."

I count out fourteen steps before I finally cave and say what's bothering me.

"They won't even look at me now. None of them. I... misjudged that situation quite poorly."

Melissa shakes her head as she lets go of my arm and shoves our bedroom door open.

"You didn't misjudge it. You were honest. There's always a risk when you tell someone how you feel."

"And I tripled the risk." I kick my boots off on the rug.

Melissa spins and winks.

"Yeah, you did. Rock and roll."

* * *

116

It's no surprise that I can't sleep on my last night in Cariadon Castle. I lie in bed, watching the shadows of the trees shift over our ceiling. Pale moonlight filters through the stained glass window whenever there's a break in the clouds, but mostly it's darkness. Shades of charcoal grey.

Our bedroom door creaks on its hinges, swinging open a few inches. A triangle of torchlight from the hall blossoms on the ceiling then disappears. The door clicks shut and soft footsteps pad over the rug.

I lay rigid in bed, heart thundering. Can a pillow be used as a weapon? I'm not built for combat.

The footsteps come to my side of the room, and I risk turning my head to squint into the gloom. The darker shadow of a man kneels at my bedside, and I stifle a squeak.

"Gigi," Lance whispers. "Are you awake?"

I huff.

"You idiot. I nearly died of fright."

I shuffle over, making space and peeling back the covers. Lance stands and slides into bed beside me. My mattress springs sing a chorus under his weight, and we both freeze, straining to listen.

Melissa snuffles on the other side of the room, turning in her bed. After what feels like a thousand years, her soft snores start up again.

"What are you doing here?" I whisper. He always looks tall, but he's so much bigger up close. His bulk takes up most of the narrow bed, his warmth spreading into my limbs. I press myself against the chilled stone wall to avoid touching him uninvited.

"Returning your visit." Lance catches my hands and presses them against his chest. His t-shirt is soft, and I can't help stroking it.

"You wouldn't look at me today."

"I'm looking at you now."

I scoff. It's pitch black. "This hardly counts."

Lance slides a palm around my waist and hitches me closer, away from the wall. Our legs tangle and our bodies press together, delicious heat washing over my skin.

"What about now?"

I flick his shoulder. "Proximity has nothing to do with it."

"It has everything to do with it. I can't think straight when you're too far away."

I frown, even though he can't see me.

"Then logic dictates you stay close, not push me aside."

Lance hums, tracing the tip of his nose from my jaw to my temple. It's cold from his walk in the night air.

"Like you said. I'm an idiot."

The storm rages outside the window, drowning out our hushed conversation. I still pause, checking for Melissa's steady breathing before running my fingertips along Lance's jaw. The day's stubble pricks at my skin, and I pull my hand back, reminded of Professor Walsh.

"You shouldn't be here."

"Why? Have you chosen one of the others?" Bitterness is thick in his voice.

"No. If I'd chosen, you'd all still look me in the eye."

Lance's arm winds tighter around my waist, pressing me closer.

"Then what's the problem?"

I don't know. What *is* the problem? It's all so messy and tangled. Asher and Lance's friendship is on the line. So are my reputation and future prospects in the department. Then there's the missing piece of Morgan; the hole jagged and painful in my chest.

"I don't want to hurt anyone."

Lance presses a kiss to the corner of my mouth. "We all know that." He leans up on one elbow, shifting to trail his lips down my throat. My breath comes faster, heat building between my legs, and I shift on the lumpy mattress.

"I still like the others. I don't want to choose at all."

"I know."

"It doesn't bother you?"

"It did at first." Lance nibbles on my earlobe, then whispers into my hair. "Now I think it's kind of hot."

My hips twitch towards him, pressing harder against his body, and Lance slides a leg between my thighs. The sudden friction against my clit makes me whimper, and I rub against him.

"That's it." Lance's hands grip my hips and roll them harder. "Show me you want me, Gigi."

I thrust faster, but the bed frame creaks. I freeze, heart pounding.

Melissa breathes evenly, deep in sleep. I surge forward and seal my mouth against his.

Lance kisses differently than Asher. He's more biting, more forceful, tightening his fist in my hair and tilting my head back for better access. I melt against him, shivering, gladly giving up the lead. I want Lance to take control. To remove the need for me to always be thinking and make me a bundle of screaming nerves.

Lance rolls on top of me, pressing me into the mattress, his hips settling between my legs. I savor the crush of his weight, the feel of him sealed against me from toe to hairline, and roll

119

my body against the hard line of his cock.

"Fuck, Gigi." Lance tears his mouth away and hangs his head, his hair tickling my cheek. We're both breathing hard, oxygen sawing out of his lungs and into mine. "I came to talk, not grind all over you."

"You started it," I grumble, and his laugh gusts over my collarbone.

"Believe me, I'm not complaining."

He kisses me again, slower this time, but no less forceful. Tension winds tighter and tighter in my core, until I'm thrusting up against him, desperate for friction. Lance pushes up on his elbow and slips a hand between us, running it down my stomach to the hem of my pajama bottoms.

"Do you want me to touch you? Make you feel good?" he grinds out against my lips.

"Yes," I gasp into his mouth.

Lance's fingers slip under the hem of my shorts and slide over the mound of my pussy. He doesn't tease like Asher; he rubs one broad finger straight down my slit, trailing back up to circle my clit. I bury my face in his neck and keen into his skin, clapping a hand over my mouth to stifle the noise.

Melissa snores gently, oblivious on the other side of the room. For a moment, the thought of Asher floats through my mind, and my heart twists in my chest. Then Lance slides a finger inside me, and my back bows against the mattress.

"Good girl." Lance strokes in and out of me, his thumb rubbing my clit. He pauses, and for a maddening second I think he's done, then he slides a second finger alongside the first.

My head thumps against the pillow, stars floating in my vision. I can just make out his features in the gloom—the sharp curve of his mouth. It spreads wider in a smirk as I thrust up to meet his fingers, forcing him deeper.

"I don't know what I expected, Gigi, but you're fucking delicious."

I whimper, screwing my eyes shut as he rubs me faster, his fingers plunging inside me. He brings me closer and closer to the brink until I teeter on the edge, every muscle in my body taut.

"Come for me," he breathes into the damp skin of my throat, and I break apart, shuddering beneath him. My thighs lock together, trapping his hand, my pussy clenching on his fingers. And Lance kisses me hard through it all, thrusting his tongue into my mouth.

Finally, I come back to my body—a sweaty, trembling heap in the middle of the bed. I force my limbs to move again, shuffling over so that Lance can collapse by my side.

His mouth is tender when he presses a kiss to my temple, and my throat goes tight. Tears well up in my eyes, and I thank God for the darkness. I'd prefer to keep this reaction to myself.

I wait for Lance to murmur goodnight and roll out of bed, but he drags me against him and holds me there. When I lean my cheek on his chest, I can hear his heart pounding almost as fast as mine.

"Let's hope you don't go walkabout tonight. I might feel used."

I burrow closer, tangling our limbs together as though I'm tethering myself to the bed, and yawn until my jaw cracks.

"Just come and fetch me back."

"Yeah, no kidding. I'll tackle you to the rug."

Chapter 9

L ance slips out of bed at first light with a kiss on my
forehead and a sheepish smile to Melissa.
"Oh, good," she says dryly, face mashed against her
pillow. "You slept here last night."

Lance grins, stretching until his shoulders pop.

"Didn't take you for a snorer, Mel."

Her pillow sails through the air, hitting Lance on the shin.

"Get out of my room, asshole."

"Wow. You're grumpy in the morning."

I burrow under the covers, muffling their bickering, and
don't come out until Lance is long gone. My stomach churns
as I shuffle upright, showing my bright red face.

"I'm sorry," I blurt before she can say anything.

Melissa snorts. "Don't worry about it. Just take it to his room
next time."

I nod, even though we're leaving today. There won't be a
next time, as far as I can tell. Last night was… an anomaly. A
statistical blip to be analyzed once I'm safely back in my lonely
dorm room.

"It feels like we've been here for years, not ten days." Melissa
dresses quickly, stuffing her things into her backpack. I do the
same, my fingers clumsy in the morning cold. "I'm almost sad

to go."

I'm definitely sad to go. This whole trip has been like a fever dream. One where people talk to me, and want to spend time with me, and I'm not Freaky Gigi anymore.

I'm not ready to leave that behind. That lonely, clammy feeling of endless nights in my dorm room slips under my skin, and I shiver.

"There's still one night at the inn," I mumble, more to myself than to Melissa, and I repeat it in my head like a mantra as we pack up the last of our stuff and strip the beds.

The door slams shut behind us as we spill into the corridor, and I flinch. It was nice while it lasted.

The others are gathered in the lobby, their voices floating along the corridor before they come into view. Melissa and I walk shoulder to shoulder, our arms brushing with every other step.

"That's weird." She frowns down the corridor. The voices are raised, urgent. "Something's happened."

I strain to pick out words, but there's just an impossible clamor, and I round the corner into the lobby none the wiser.

The group's luggage is piled in the center of the room: a heap of brightly colored backpacks on the rug. Annabelle, Thabo, Asher and Lance sit on the sofas, tapping at their phones or murmuring to each other. Morgan paces along the edge of the lobby, talking on the phone and raking his hand through his hair whenever it cuts out. And Professor Walsh towers over the caretaker by the door, shouting and flinging an arm towards the exit.

"Oh, boy." Melissa drops her backpack on the pile and walks straight to Lance and Asher. She drops in neatly between them, clapping them both on the knee. I hover for a second,

123

torn between where I want to be and where will be less uncomfortable.

My cowardice wins out. I add my backpack to the heap and go to sit cross-legged in front of the hearth.

There's no room on these sofas. And I am not the type of person who can just yell for people to make space. I hitch my legs up in front of me and rest my chin on my knees.

Morgan paces the length of the lobby again, calling into the phone over and over. He frowns and pinches the bridge of his nose—that's his headache face. Professor Walsh's voice rings through the lobby, ranting about urgent meetings and flights, but I block him out and crawl to my backpack. I screw my eyes shut as I rummage for the little cardboard box. They're all so loud. It's too much to process.

"Here." I push to my feet and step into Morgan's path, holding out a bottle of water and two aspirin. He stares at them, eye flicking up to mine, before he takes them with muttered thanks. He tosses his head back to swallow the pills, his throat working, and I watch it with a crease between my eyes.

Morgan hands back the bottle and I retreat to my spot on the rug. I don't know what all the panic is about, but suddenly I'm eager to go home too.

I miss my dorm room. The silence. The simplicity.

Professor Walsh pauses for breath in his rant, and Mr Evans lets out a raspy chuckle.

"See for yourself," he says, then tugs the door open. Snowflakes billow into the room, melting in the heat from the fire and pattering onto the flagstones. Where the path should lead away from the castle is a five-foot wall of snow. "I'll fetch you a shovel," he tells the professor, then cracks up in wheezing laughter.

Professor Walsh looks like he might give the elderly caretaker a thump. Morgan strides between them, his face pale as he takes in the snowdrift.

"Signal's patchy. We might have better luck from the ramparts."

"Just deal with it, Morgan," Professor Walsh spits, like his graduate student is somehow at fault for the weather. "Now."

He strides out of the lobby. Morgan watches him go, his knuckles white around his phone, and I grimace when his eyes fall to me.

Guess we're going nowhere soon. I'm going to need more aspirin.

* * *

Here is a list of things we lost in the night: Electricity. Hot water. Any hope of making our flights. The last shreds of respect for Professor Walsh.

Here is what we gained: Five feet of snow. And a migraine for Morgan.

"Come on, Gigi. Don't be a wet blanket."

I glance at Melissa over my glasses.

"That saying makes no sense."

"You've spent this whole trip studying. That deadline's not for weeks. What will you remember more: exploring in the snow, or hunching over your laptop?"

I've spent many a sweet hour hunched over my laptop, but I see her point. Plus, three hours of staring at my screen have strained my eyes. I pull off my glasses, rubbing at them with a sigh.

"Fine. But I'm hardly a mountaineer."

Melissa tugs me from my library chair. "Color me shocked."

In the time I've been working in the library alone, honing my research paper, the others have dug a narrow path from the castle entrance out into the snow. I bundle up before joining them, tugging on my woolly hat and mittens.

The Welsh mountains may not be the Himalayas, but they still claim a body count each year. No need to get cocky.

Annabelle and Thabo are already outside, visible through the doorway. They fling snowballs at each other, shrieking loud enough to trigger an avalanche, and I wince at all the noise.

Asher and Lance hover by the doorway. Lance winks at me while Asher stares at the ground.

Morgan's nowhere to be seen. Neither is Professor Walsh, but that's a gift rather than a concern.

"What's the plan?" I plant myself in front of Asher, hoping he'll look at me. He doesn't. But he does frown at the rug when Lance grabs my hand and tugs me through the door.

"No plan, Gigi. Time to let your hair down."

My hair is already loose beneath my hat, but I don't bother to correct Lance. I let him drag me out into the snow, the pine-fresh air nipping at my bare cheeks. The wind whistles over the mountainside, ruffling branches and knocking the top off snow drifts. Our boots sink as we wade, knee-deep, squinting against the glare of sunshine on the white landscape.

Lance stops me fifteen feet from the door and spins me around. His arm settles around my neck, heavy and warm, and he ducks his head to murmur in my ear.

"This is kind of like research, right? It must have snowed back in the day."

The thought warms me, and I stifle a grin.

"You make a good point."

126

Looking back at the castle, heaped with snow, I can picture it hundreds of years ago. There was no electricity to lose; the wood stores were well-prepared to heat the castle, and the nearby stream would provide water. The larder was stocked for months at a time, the castle's inhabitants settling in for the long haul. I can practically taste the wood smoke; hear the crackling great fires.

I wonder if they ever ventured into the snow just to get some space. I bet they did.

A dark shape moves on the ramparts, pacing back and forth. Morgan. My mouth suddenly dry, I turn away from the mossy keep with its snowy turrets.

Asher squeezes past us on the narrow path, his cheeks flushed and his eyes glued to his boots. My hand twitches out, reaching for him, but I snatch it back. I won't push where I'm not wanted.

I won't chase any of these men. I told them how I felt, laid myself bare. They can do whatever they want with that information.

I have no illusions about the chances of three gorgeous men being so into me they're willing to share.

Well. Apart from one, maybe. Lance nibbles on my earlobe before taking hold of my mitten. He drags me after Asher, my steps clumsy in the snow, as Melissa trails behind all three of us.

I throw a helpless look over my shoulder. She raises an eyebrow and smirks.

"Don't pretend you hate this," she calls, loud enough that a crow bursts out of a tree. Over her shoulder, the dark shape on the ramparts stills. "One down, two to go."

I bug my eyes out at her, willing her to shut the hell up, then

127

turn back when I nearly face-plant a boulder. Lance pulls me around it, tugging me after Asher's retreating back.

"Get a move on, Gigi," he mutters, quiet so only I can hear. "I'm trying to set you up."

My body flushes hot under my coat, half from embarrassment, and half because his words turn me on. I clear my throat.

"He won't want me if I'm a sweaty mess."

Lance throws me a look over his shoulder, his gaze raking me from my soaking boots to my wind-tangled hair.

"Asher's not a fucking moron. Give him some credit."

* * *

Asher rounds the outside of the castle and beats a path up the mountainside. The snow lies in great drifts, gathered around the bases of trees and against the castle walls. I follow, sweating and puffing, aiming my footsteps at the holes from Asher's boot prints.

"Slow down!"

Asher doesn't turn his head. He keeps forging upwards, his head bowed, his arms swinging. But maybe he does slow down a tiny bit.

We leave Lance and Melissa bickering by the castle walls, Melissa shrieking as Lance empties a snowball down her jacket. Still, Asher doesn't turn around, his thighs flexing as he plunges up the incline, quick and powerful. I lean against a tree trunk, my mitten snagging on the rough bark, and suck in several deep breaths.

Screw this.

"Asher!" I yell. "Don't be an asshole. Your legs are really fucking long."

Finally, he grinds to a halt, his black winter jacket stark against the snow. Turning in place, Asher folds his arms and waits as I wheeze the last few feet up to him.

"Don't even think about it," I gasp, clutching a handful of his sleeve. "You can wait for two more minutes."

Asher's mouth twists, his cheeks slapped pink by the wind. He didn't bother with a hat, and his blond hair lifts with the breeze.

"Sorry," he says quietly. "I was distracted."

"By?"

Asher shrugs. "My thoughts."

It's such a supremely unhelpful answer that I can't help but wheeze out a laugh. Asher smiles too, a faint curl of his mouth, and my pounding heart squeezes in my chest.

I'm so affected by the climb that it's frankly embarrassing. Making a mental note to add cardiovascular exercise to my routine back at campus, I close my eyes and suck in long, slow breaths. I hold them for the count of ten, then gust them out, eyes screwed shut.

"Are you afraid of heights?" A warm hand clasps my elbow.

"No. Just my own lack of fitness."

Still, Asher doesn't move his hand, and I lean into him by an inch. When I open my eyes, I'm struck by the weird thought that the mountains suit Asher. The bright snow matches his teeth, and the sunny blue skies are like his eyes. His face is built from sharp planes, like the sheer rock in the mountainside, and he always smells like the pine-fresh wind.

Asher raises his eyebrows, and I shake my head like I can rattle those thoughts loose.

It's weird enough to stalk someone up a mountain. If I share these little observations, I'm just asking for some kind of diagnosis.

Asher jerks his chin over my shoulder, and I turn around on wobbly feet. We're on eye level with the castle ramparts, looking down on the tops of trees. From up here, Melissa and Lance are small creatures in the snow, and the castle looks bigger. Sprawling.

A figure raises a hand on the ramparts. Morgan. I bite my lip and wave a mitten back.

"You picked Lance, then?" Asher blurts. "And Morgan didn't give you a hard time?"

"Unlike you, you mean?" Asher looks sheepish when I square off with him. "No, I didn't pick Lance. Why does everyone keep asking me that?"

Honestly, it's not a difficult concept. I want all three of them. At the same time.

It might be unreasonable. Or fantastical, like those stories. But it's not complicated math.

"So he's okay with you liking other guys?" Asher sounds doubtful.

"Apparently so. Lance is more evolved than I gave him credit for."

"And… you do. Still like us, too."

I sigh. "I won't hassle you, Asher. Either you want this or you don't. Lance and I are both in."

"What about Morgan?"

I watch the dark figure tracking back and forth along the ramparts. His head is bent, a phone clutched to his ear, and I can practically see the frustration rolling off him in waves.

"He's not interested."

Asher grunts, then nudges me gently.

"I'm sorry, Gigi."

I shrug. What is there to say? I knew my chances were slim. And Asher looks so sympathetic it's making me itch.

At least no one knows about how I threw myself at Morgan in the dungeon. That, at least, is a small mercy.

"It's fine." I try to sound like I mean it. "And it's fine if you don't want this either. I hope we can still be friends, at least."

Asher gives me his first genuine smile of the day, and it warms me from the inside out.

"Always, Gigi. You can count on that."

* * *

My feet are cold. They lead me along corridors of icy flagstones, each turn carrying me closer. I walk down the center of the rug whenever there is one, but sometimes it's just my bare skin against the stone. Goosebumps prickle along my arms, my nipples pebbling under my t-shirt. The wind moans outside.

The door swings open easily, smooth on its hinges. The room is dark, the fire banked low in the hearth, and I veer towards the closest bed. The door clicks shut behind me, muffling the howl of the wind.

Two sets of breathing. Blond hair splayed across a pillow. I peel back the covers and slide into the warmth.

"What the... shit. Lance!"

Across the room, there's a thump and a string of curses. I rest my cheek against the pillow and stare straight ahead at a bare, muscled chest. Footsteps thud across the flagstones, then a hand clamps onto my shoulder. It starts to pull me onto my back, but another arms shoots out and stops it.

"Careful! Don't wake her."

A sigh gusts over my cheek from behind.

131

"We've got to start locking that door."

"Shut up. You're just pissed she got in my bed."

There's a grunt, then a chuckle beside me. Gentle fingers dance over my cheek, brushing my hair behind my ear.

"How do you like it, asshole?"

"I'd like it more if you'd make some fucking room."

"Seriously?"

Deadly silence echoes around the stone walls. In the fireplace, the embers crackle. Without a word, the man next to me shuffles back against the wall, taking his warmth with him. Steady hands guide me as I follow him, inching closer on the lumpy mattress until I'm plastered against his chest. I can hear his racing heartbeat; feel the gust of his breath tickling my forehead.

Bliss.

The bed dips and a body slides in behind me, curving against my back. I was wrong; this is what heaven feels like. Two muscled chests, two sets of strong arms winding around me. I press my icy toes against the bare legs behind me, and the man sucks in a sharp breath.

"What?" The man in front of me sounds wary.

"Her feet are fucking freezing."

He relaxes, the tension bleeding out of his muscles, and he tucks my head under his chin.

"You deal with her feet, then. I'll take charge of this end."

* * *

I wake up in an inferno. My bangs stick to my forehead; the backs of my knees are damp with sweat. I try to roll onto my back, but I bump against something. I go forward, but it's the same problem.

"It's a twin bed, Gigi. You're trapped forever."

Lance's voice tickles my ear. I blink my eyes open, squinting at the face next to mine on the pillow.

A very blurry Asher smiles at me. At least, I'm ninety percent sure it's him.

"Um." I clear my throat. "I don't have my glasses. Is that you, Asher?"

He chuckles, and I relax at the sound. It's definitely him. Lance whistles and lurches out of bed behind me, letting in a flood of cold air.

"You're as blind as a fucking bat." His footsteps thud across the floor and the door slams shut behind him. I tamp down my disappointment that he's gone already. It's hardly reasonable. I wasn't invited, after all.

"I'm sorry I came here again," I whisper. "I don't control where I go."

Asher's face shifts, and his voice drops low.

"I'd rather you came here than anywhere else."

For a second, I imagine sleepwalking into someone else's room—Thabo's, or God forbid, Professor Walsh's. I shudder, pressing closer to Asher's chest.

Sleepwalkers are vulnerable. There's a reason I double lock my dorm room.

Even though I trust Asher, I shouldn't be here either. Not really. Ignoring the way my heart throbs in protest, I start to untangle our limbs.

"You don't have to go." Asher's voice is rough. His arm winds tighter around my waist. "You can stay if you like."

The door bangs open before I can answer, thudding off the wall, and Lance strides back to the bedside. He slides my glasses on with careful hands, and winks once I can see him again. The

133

mattress creaks as he climbs back in behind me.

Right. Okay. Two men in a bed. This is a lot to process.

I guess I knew what I was proposing when I said I wanted all of them, but the reality is more daunting than the theory. They're both so big, dwarfing me between them, and their palms are huge as they stroke my side.

"So tense." Lance nips my earlobe. "Are you having second thoughts, Gigi?"

I focus on Asher's dimple while I catch my breath, pressing a fingertip against the indent.

"No. Not second thoughts. Just considering logistics."

Lance chuckles, but the sound fades away when Asher leans forward and presses his lips against mine. He's tentative—like it's our first kiss all over again—and I sigh into his mouth.

It was like missing a limb, having him with me then snatched away. My pulse calms for the first time in days, molten heat spreading through my body. I nibble on Asher's lip, lazy and decadent, and he shifts so his hips press against mine.

He's hard. He wants me—wants this too.

"Are you sure?" I mumble.

Asher cups my jaw and kisses me harder. Lance unleashes a shuddering breath, sealing himself against my back. The firm line of his cock nudges my spine, and I grind back against him.

It's so much. It's perfect.

Their hands scorch me as they drift over my skin. It's overwhelming and it's not enough, and I whimper as Asher tugs my t-shirt over my head. Lance's fingers hook in the waistband of my shorts, teasing them down my thighs. I draw my feet up, kicking my shorts off into the muddle of covers at the bottom of the bed.

Yes. More.

I could die happy pressed between their hot, bare skin. My eyes drift closed as they both kick off their boxers, sealing back against me without a single scrap of fabric between us. It's sensory overload, but in the best possible way. Every glimpse of toned chest, every pulse of heat, every sniff of their masculine scent. I lean forward, eyes still shut, and lick a stripe up the center of Asher's chest.

Salty. Delicious.

Asher laughs, the sound rumbling through his rib cage, and I shift to scrape my teeth over his throat instead. My glasses knock against my forehead, knocked askew, and I huff.

"I'm done with these." I tug them off and pass them back to Lance without looking. He plucks them from my hand, places them on the bedside cabinet, then swats my ass. The sting spreads hot over my skin, and I squirm.

"So ungrateful."

"They're impractical for this activity." God, I hope I don't sound as breathless as I feel. "And I know who I'm with, now."

"I should fucking hope so," Lance grumbles, but he shuffles close again, thrusting gently against my thigh. I roll my body between them, rubbing against them both in one motion, then smirk when they let out matching groans.

This isn't so hard.

For two naked guys sandwiching me in bed, they're weirdly cautious. They both hang back, nibbling my neck or sucking on my bottom lip, hands drifting idly over my side and down my thigh. When their hands brush by accident, they don't jerk away, but they both swerve to avoid each other. And with every second they don't touch me where I need, the tension in my core ratchets tighter until I'm keening with frustration.

My head thumps back against Lance's collarbone.

"Are you kidding me? You're driving me mad. This must be some kind of joke."

Asher hums and nibbles his way down my chest before taking my nipple between his teeth. I gasp, arching against his mouth as he sucks on me, swirling his tongue. I bury my hand in his soft hair, gripping a fistful and holding him there.

"Give us a break, Gigi," Lance murmurs in my ear. "We're new to this, too."

Guilty, I let go of Asher's hair, but he shakes his head and sucks me harder. I grip him again, giving a sharp tug, and Asher moans against my breast. He thrusts against my hip, hard, and the head of his cock slides over my skin.

A steady palm creeps over my waist towards my core. I hitch a leg up over Asher's hip, breathing hard, as Lance's fingers tease my soaked pussy. He circles my clit, pinching lightly, then dips into my entrance.

Enough. Enough teasing. I'm wound so tight, my teeth are chattering. Craning my neck back, I nudge Lance with my forehead.

"Lance. Condoms."

He rolls over, grumbling, and there's the sound of a backpack zip. Cold air washes over my back where he was a second ago, and a string of curses line up ready on my tongue. But then he's back, his heat searing my skin, and I swallow the words as a foil wrapper drops onto the bed covers.

Asher plucks it off the sheets, his mouth leaving my wet nipple to the chill morning air. I huff at the lack of contact, their hands busy, even though they're doing what I asked them to. My clit throbs with every beat of my racing pulse, and if I don't feel one of them inside me right this instant, I'm going to scream.

"Ready?" Asher murmurs, his forehead resting against mine. He grips my thigh and hitches me higher. The head of his cock nudges at my entrance, and I dig my nails into his shoulders.

"Asher Penderly, if you don't fuck me in the next three seconds—"

He pushes inside me in one stroke. I groan, my head falling back against Lance's shoulder, as Asher pulls all the way out, then thrusts in again. Reaching blindly behind me, I find Lance's hand then clutch it to my chest.

"Touch me."

He squeezes my breast, then pinches my nipple.

"Fuck," Asher grinds out, his gaze fixed on his best friend's hand on my breast. He fucks me harder, slamming deep inside, and I hiss with satisfaction. "That's really hot."

Lance sucks a bruise onto my neck, then pulls away just enough to speak, his words vibrating into my skin.

"That's what I've been trying to tell you."

I wind my hand into Lance's hair and say nothing. I can't speak. It's all I can do to hold on to them both, Asher thrusting me back against Lance's chest. Lance reaches over me to grip Asher's hip with one hand, holding us all tight together, and the extra friction catches my clit in just the right way.

"God."

My limbs start to shake, my fingers tugging at Lance's hair. Asher thrusts deep inside me, filling me up, and the tension in my core snaps.

I break. Pleasure rolls through me in waves, and I clamp down on Asher's cock. He curses, swelling inside me then coming with a shout. Lance holds us both through it all, my head tucked under his chin.

Asher has barely pulled out before I'm scrabbling behind me

for Lance.

"I'm here," he murmurs in my ear. "I've got you."

He slides into my pussy, grip tight on my hip. Asher fucked me back against Lance's chest; now Lance fucks me onto Asher. He practically crawls on top of us, pounding me into the bed, and Asher muffles my cries with his mouth. He cradles my jaw, kissing me deep and slow, and the contrast drives me out of my mind.

Lance smacks my ass, and I groan, sucking on Asher's tongue.

"Fuck," Lance mutters behind us. "You're so fucking gorgeous, Gigi."

Asher hums in agreement, his thumbs rubbing along my jaw. I screw my eyes shut, so overwhelmed with sensation as these two men make my body sing. I clench my teeth so tight when I come, it's a wonder my molars don't crack.

I slump against Asher as Lance collapses behind me, chest heaving. They each run soothing palms over my sides, my muscles still twitching.

"That was nice," I mumble into the bed sheets once I can string a sentence together.

Asher chuckles, and Lance tugs the bed covers over the sweat cooling on our skin.

"Always knew you'd be a harsh grader, Gigi. Understatement of the century."

Chapter 10

There are worse places to be trapped in a power cut than a fully functional castle. The torches lining the corridors may be ornamental most days, but now they're our main source of light. And though there's no hot water, the fireplaces in each room keep us from freezing solid.

I still risk a shower, dancing in and out of the icy spray, sluicing off the evidence of my morning with Lance and Asher. By the time I find the others sprawled over the armchairs in the library, my lips have turned blue.

"Come here."

Asher opens his arms as soon I walk through the door. I make a beeline straight for him, curling up on his lap and burrowing into his sweater. Lance grins at me from where he's sat with Melissa, each of them perched on an arm of the sofa.

"You took a shower, Gigi? Why, were you dirty?"

"Shut up."

"Ignore him," Asher murmurs into my damp hair.

"Yes, please ignore him," Melissa mutters, turning the page of a hardback book. "There's a backlog for my therapist as it is."

Morgan strides through the door, only slowing a little when he sees us, then heads to the spare armchair and throws himself down. His dark hair is rumpled, and the shadows under his eyes look like bruises. My chest aches, and I clutch handfuls of Asher's sweater to stop myself going to him.

"No luck?" Lance says, and I thank God someone else asked the question. Morgan's clear exhaustion has been playing on my mind, but he's made it clear that he doesn't want to speak to me.

"Nope." Morgan leans back, resting his head on the armchair as his eyes drift shut. "Anyone who might have helped probably changed their minds the second Walsh started yelling down the phone."

"We're stuck here, then," Melissa says flatly.

Morgan shrugs. "For a day or two. The snow will melt soon enough."

Melissa and Asher start murmuring about their plans to visit home before the semester. Cancelled flights; disappointed parents. Even Lance sighs, chewing the inside of his cheek, and it occurs to me that I'm the only one who won't be missed while we're here.

I sent my parents their bi-weekly email the evening before the power cut. They won't even notice anything is wrong for twelve more days.

Asher chafes my arms, then tugs a blanket from the back of the armchair and wraps it around me.

"Does it bother you?" he asks.

Does what bother me: Being snowed in? Being cold? Missing flights? Or my complete and tragic lack of a social life?

"Nope." I echo Morgan, my eyes on the older man as I snuggle into Asher. "I like it here."

Forty minutes later, I am eighty percent sure that Morgan

has another migraine. He hasn't opened his eyes since he rested his head back, but his chest is rising and falling too quickly for him to be asleep. Every now and then, he frowns blindly at the ceiling, until finally I can't take it anymore.

"Be right back." I slide off Asher's lap and set off for the kitchens. It takes a while to hunt through the cupboards, and since there's no power I have to light the gas hob with a match. But I return with a packet of aspirin and a steaming mug of ginger tea.

Morgan doesn't stir when I pause at his side. I chew my lip, then drag a stool over.

"Ginger is good for nausea." I place the mug down with a thunk. He doesn't open his eyes, though I know damn well he hears me. "Give it a minute to cool."

I tuck the aspirin next to the mug and turn to go back to Asher, but a hand catches my elbow.

"Thank you." Exhausted eyes hold mine. "You didn't have to do that."

I nod, because that is an obvious statement. No one is forced to make ginger tea.

"Feel better," I say, then feeling brave, I pet his hair quickly before moving away. Lance and Asher both watch me, eyes tracking my progress across the room, but Asher smiles when I climb back onto his lap.

"He'll come around." The words are soft in my ear. I shake my head.

"Not this time."

The fire pops, sparks showering the flagstones, and I burrow under Asher's chin. Lance watches me watching Morgan, stroking his lip, and the wind moans outside the castle walls.

* * *

"Oh my god."

Melissa holds up her book, glancing from the pages to Lance, then Asher, then me. Then she tosses back her head and cackles, the book dropping into her lap.

"What?" Lance grunts, stretched out on the sofa, an arm tossed over his face. His study notes are scattered over the floor, abandoned. Melissa ignores him, sliding off her armrest and crossing to Morgan.

"Look at this." Morgan squints blearily at the pages shoved in his face. His eyes scan back and forth, a frown creasing his forehead, until understanding dawns.

"Uncanny." He offers Melissa a weak smile and a nod, settling back with a sigh when she turns away.

"What is it?" Asher asks as Melissa brings the book to us. It's a hefty, leather bound tome, the sort that snobby people line their bookshelves with but never read. The spine creaks as Melissa lays it in my lap.

"It's creepy, is what it is."

The pages are covered in smudgy cursive writing, unreadable at first glance. In one corner, an illustration dominates the page: an old-fashioned drawing in black and colored inks.

A king on a throne.

A queen at his side, holding his hand even as her gaze tracks to another.

And standing nearby, a handsome knight, stealing the queen's attention.

"King Arthur, Lancelot and Guinevere," I list off immediately. "So? They're hardly the most exciting local legend."

"Look at their faces, Gigi."

I lean closer, frowning. There's... something familiar, I suppose. In the king's bright blue eyes, and the knight's knowing smirk.

"It's called cognitive bias." I settle back against Asher. "You see what you want to see."

"You're no fun." Melissa snatches the book back and wanders over to Lance. He peels his arm off his forehead and stares at the drawing, eyebrows raised.

"I dunno, Gigi. That knight's a looker. And the queen looks like a right know-it-all."

I scoff, but it's Asher who pipes up.

"If that's us, then where's Morgan?"

An awkward hush falls over the room. Our tutor frowns at the ceiling, but doesn't open his eyes.

"King Arthur had an adviser." Melissa chooses her words carefully. "He's not in the drawing, but he's in all the stories. An older, wiser man called Merlin."

Lance bursts out laughing, and the sound almost covers Morgan's mutter.

"Not *that* much older."

A roar echoes down the corridor and we all cringe, wincing at the floor. It's been like this all day—quiet for a stretch, then Professor Walsh throws a temper tantrum. And each time, poor Morgan has to drag himself out there so the professor has someone to yell at.

The sigh that comes out of Morgan sounds like he's dredged from the bottom of his chest.

"Here we go again." He braces his hands on the armrests, but Melissa drops her book in his lap.

"I'll go. Throw some charm at the professor. It's too fraught in here, anyway."

She throws me a wink on her way out to soften her words, leaving me alone with all three guys. It's the first time we've been alone for days—the first time since my awkward confession.

I wonder whether Morgan knows what I did with the others this morning. Whether the idea turns him on. I shift, my cheeks staining pink.

"I'll go see if she needs help." I lurch out of Asher's lap before he feels me squirm.

The Guinevere in the drawing looks so regal. So sure of herself. *Must be nice*, I think to myself as I trip on the edge of the rug.

* * *

Somehow, in the five minutes between Melissa leaving the library and my stumbling out the doorway, I lose track of her. There are no signs of life in Professor Walsh's makeshift office when I stick my head around the door. There's no tinkle of china in the kitchen, and the only bodies slumped in the lobby are Annabelle and Thabo napping on the leather sofas.

I wander through the corridors, straining my ears for the rumble of conversation. The echo of my footsteps on the stone and the wind whistling down the stairwells are the only sounds.

Weird. You can usually hear the professor half a mile away.

A high-pitched laugh echoes down a corridor to my left, and I veer towards it. The torches gutter on the walls, the firelight weak compared to the shafts of daylight streaming through the stained glass windows.

A low voice rumbles, and I hear my name, followed by another feminine laugh. My stomach flips, my mouth suddenly dry, but I keep walking. I'm used to people laughing at me.

When I reach the door to the room with the voices, I lift my fist, but something holds me back. I wait, my heart thundering in my ears, my breath coming short.

"Here, baby." The voice is clear through the wooden door. So is the sharp intake of breath.

I reel back, bile creeping up my throat. Melissa and Professor Walsh? I hurry back along the corridor the way I came, trying to scrub the mental image from my mind. And even though it's none of my business who Melissa sleeps with, my chest burns with something like betrayal.

He's so cruel. To everyone, but especially to me.

I stick to the rugs whenever I can, the fabric muffling my footsteps. I only slow my stride when I reach the kitchens and a horrible thought occurs to me.

Incomplete data. That is what I have. I heard two words, then drew my own conclusions.

What did I just tell the others? Cognitive bias. I heard what I wanted to hear. Not that I *want* my new friend to be involved with such a creep, but the alternative is so much worse...

I turn on my heel and sprint back down the corridor. My boots clatter against the flagstones, and my hair streams behind me as I run. I'm going so fast I overshoot the door and nearly topple over trying to change direction.

The heavy door slams against the wall, and I burst into the room. I pant, unable to speak, as I take in the professor's red face and Melissa's pale one. She's backed against a table, her palms up, with the professor's leg shoved between her thighs.

Her fingers are trembling. She's chalky white. I am one hundred percent sure of what I'm doing.

"Melissa. Come here." I stretch out a hand, glaring at

Professor Walsh. He doesn't even look ashamed; just annoyed that I've interrupted. "I need your help in the other room."

He clamps a hand down on my roommate's shoulder.

"She'll be there in a minute. Run along, Gigi."

I suck in a deep breath.

"I need her now, *sir*." I pour all my loathing into that word. I want him to know how little I think of him. Melissa wriggles, trying to slide out from in front of him, but Professor Walsh cages her in place.

No. I may not understand all social interactions, but I know this is horribly wrong. I raise my chin and look him right in the eye.

"I won't leave without her."

Rage flashes over Professor Walsh's face, then he smooths it away as soon as it came. He steps back, tucking his hands in his pockets and smiling like this was all a misunderstanding. His handsome face is untroubled; his shoulders relaxed.

"So dramatic, Gigi. You know, this kind of disrespect will show in your final grade."

I roll my eyes and tell him, "Fuck your grade," then gesture for Melissa again. She lurches across the room on unsteady legs, gripping my hand hard when she reaches me. I don't hang around to hear his reply; I clamp Melissa's arm under mine and drag her out the door.

The corridors are a blur, our steps unsteady. We pull each other along in a panicked daze. My heart doesn't start to slow until our bedroom door clicks shut and we're truly alone.

It takes almost fifteen minutes, but we push the mahogany chest of drawers in front of the door, scraping it over the flagstones. The only window in our room is high on the wall, too small for a grown man to fit through. Safely barricaded, we look at each other, breathing hard and eyes wide. The horror of what just happened gnaws at my brain, muddling my thoughts.

There are things I should say. Comforts I should give. A normal person would know how to deal with this.

Then Melissa's face crumples, and my chest caves in.

* * *

No one in their right mind would call for Gigi Russell in an emotional emergency. It's not that I don't care—I care very deeply. In fact, I care so much that it renders me useless. I see someone in pain, and it's like that distress wafts off them in waves and reverberates through me, too.

So, Melissa bursts into tears.

And I lose my shit.

"No, no no no," I mumble to myself, lurching towards her then patting her awkwardly on the shoulder. Melissa wraps her arms around herself, gripping her elbows and bending over at the waist. Huge sobs wrack her body, scouring out her chest, and my own heart constricts in response.

I can't breathe.

"There, there." Have I always been such an idiot? I rest my arm gingerly around her shoulders, and Melissa slumps into me. Her sudden weight knocks me sideways, and I stagger before I right myself. Melissa just sways with me, oblivious and lost in herself. I guide us to the edge of her bed, easing her down to sit on the mattress.

"You're safe in here," I babble, "and he is a disgusting excuse for a man. We'll report him, I promise, and until then you'll never be alone with him again."

I stroke her hair as I talk, fuzzy little strands that have curled free from her braids. It's freezing in here, our hearth empty, and I weigh the relative importance of lighting the fire versus immediate social support.

A shiver runs through me, juddering my limbs, and I reach behind us to tug the bed covers around our shoulders. Melissa hiccups, gripping the blankets, and curls closer into my side. Social support it is.

Before this trip, I estimate I was touched by another person approximately once a month. Less, even, if I take polite handshakes out of the equation. My parents have been known to hug me once or twice, and some of the frat boys on campus clap me on the shoulder when they call me Freaky Gigi.

It's… an adjustment. First Asher, Lance and Morgan, and now Melissa. A very different sort of touch, obviously, but one that somehow feels even more delicate. I do not want to get this wrong.

Melissa draws in a shuddering breath, wiping the bed covers under her nose. She's staring at her feet, her face oddly blank, and I know I'm missing something here. It's like sitting a test I haven't studied for.

"Um. Are you all right?"

She finally looks at me, turning her head slowly and frowning at me. Not like she's mad, but like she forgot I was here.

"It's my fault," she whispers.

Ah. I know the answer to this one.

"Definitely not. One hundred percent. This is all on Professor Walsh."

"I flirted with him, and I let him lead me off to another room, and when he cornered me against that table my mind went blank and I couldn't fucking think—"

148

I grip her shoulder, hard.

"It's not your fault. Even I know that, and I offend people all the time. If I know he was wrong, he does too. Don't you think?"

Melissa chews on her lip, considering my words, then the rigidity bleeds out of her. She cants to the side, her head resting on my shoulder, and mumbles into the space below my chin.

"It sucks there's no hot water. I need a thousand hot showers to wash that creep off me."

I hum. "We could roll in the snow."

Melissa snorts, and something wet drips in my lap. She dabs at it with the bed covers, and I opt not to say anything.

Footsteps echo past our bedroom door and we both freeze, silent except for our breathing. The steps fade away down the corridor, and we relax again, slumping on the bed.

"I don't want to go back out there."

I pat her shoulder. "Neither do I."

"So let's stay here, then."

"Okay."

We can miss dinner. It's only one meal. And if anyone comes looking for us, our chest of drawers will block the way. We shuffle back and lay on Melissa's bed, each lost in our own thoughts.

Tomorrow, we've been told we'll attempt the hike down the mountain in the snow. I soothe my racing heart with images of the professor falling to his death in a crevasse.

Chapter 11

We set out early, before the blue tinge of dawn has washed out of the sky. What was a six-hour hike on the way here will take us hours longer today—we're going downhill, yes, but through endless drifts of half-melted snow and ice. Swaddled in winter layers, with our backpacks wobbling on our shoulders, we wave goodbye to Mr Evans and file down the mountain path.

It takes less than twenty steps for me to slip, my heel sliding on a patch of ice. Lance catches my elbow and sets me upright.

"Careful," he mutters. There are no jokes this morning. Not since Melissa told Asher and Lance what happened last night in hushed, stilted whispers. The two men were ready to tear the professor apart with their bare hands, but we calmed them down long enough to see reason.

We have no proof. Not yet. And no way will the college board believe us over a tenured professor. If Asher and Lance charge in and beat Walsh to a pulp, the only outcome will be their asses getting kicked out of college.

No. Melissa and I agreed: we need to take this creep down.

Asher sticks close to his sister's side, glaring daggers at Professor Walsh's back. Either the professor is oblivious to the surrounding tension this morning or he is so supremely unthreatened that it amuses him. He was in a great mood over breakfast, cracking jokes and needling Morgan.

Melissa has barely said a word since last night.

"Damn it." I skid and right myself again, arms stretched out to help me balance. I am no athlete at the best of times, and it's hard going on the snowy path. Before long, my thighs burn and my joints rattle with every step, and Lance slowly drifts ahead.

"Something's wrong." Morgan's voice at my elbow makes me jump, and I place a hand on a tree trunk to steady myself. Our tutor frowns down at me, his cheeks glowing bright from the icy mountain breeze.

His jacket and hiking pants are both black, and his gray eyes are stormy. His collar is open at the throat, showing a triangle of pale, smooth skin.

"Do you need help?" I'm not sure why he's come to me, but I'll certainly try my best.

"No." Morgan takes my arm and pulls me along, the rest of the group getting smaller up ahead in the trees. "Something is wrong with you. Something's happened."

"Oh. Yeah."

I watch my feet, taking care to step in ready-made boot prints. There are lots to choose from at the back of the line, but I still end up weaving all over the path. Morgan keeps level with me, his hand clamped around my forearm.

"You're killing me here, Gigi."

I glance up at him.

"Sorry. I'm going as fast as I can."

"No, not—"

Morgan breaks off and pinches the bridge of his nose. I pull a face at my boots. Morgan takes a long breath, then tries again.

"Not that. Please tell me what's wrong."

I wrinkle my nose, grabbing a nearby branch to help lower myself down a big step.

"It's not project-related."

"All right."

"It's personal."

"Okay."

"You won't like it."

Morgan inhales sharply. "For f—please, Gigi."

I let go of the branch and brush green needles off my mitten.

"Professor Walsh tried to kiss Melissa last night."

Morgan says nothing, and I glance up at him. He's pale, his mouth pressed in a firm line. His grip tightens on my forearm until I tap the back of his hand and he eases off.

"I'll deal with it," he says shortly, but I'm already shaking my head.

"We have a plan."

"You have a—like hell—you're not dealing with this. I mean it, Gigi. Stay far away from him."

Morgan jerks my arm as he speaks, lowering his face until it's inches from mine. I appreciate the slightly deranged look in his eyes, but it doesn't change anything.

"No, thank you. But we will take proper precautions."

"That was an order, Gigi."

I snort. "You're a tutor, not a drill sergeant. I told you because you asked, not because I wanted input." I can't stop the bitterness tinging my voice. "Like you said, our relationship is professional. This is a personal matter."

Morgan's face is strained, but he keeps going.

"It's college-related. I will deal with it."

"We don't need your help."

152

"Tough shit. You're getting it."

I blow out an angry breath, fluttering my bangs and fogging my glasses. Nearby, a squirrel skitters up a tree. I weave around a boulder half-blocking the path, muttering to myself about never telling Morgan anything again.

"Gigi." Morgan tugs me to a halt, pushing me back against the boulder. The coat of moss draped over the stone cushions my backpack. "I'm not trying to upset you. I'm trying to protect you. Do you understand that?"

I focus on the zip on Morgan's left pocket. He gives me a little shake.

"Yes," I grind out. "I'm still not telling you personal things again."

Morgan looks pained, but he nods.

"Fine. I won't ask you to."

It's the exact opposite of what I want him to say. I chew on the inside of my cheek, mood sour.

"This is why," Morgan blurts. I blink up at him. "This is why we can't be… more. I'd be no better than Professor Walsh."

"But Walsh is gross," I say slowly, confused. "And I want you too." Morgan wouldn't have to trap me in a room and cage me against a desk. If I could, I'd sit on his lap at breakfast.

Morgan sighs. "It's still wrong."

I open my mouth to argue, but he tugs me away from the boulder and after the group.

It's not the same. I know that down to my bones. Morgan's not decades older than me; he's not in charge of our grades. And he'd never make me feel like Melissa felt last night.

Up in the branches, a bird screams.

I'm inclined to agree.

* * *

The sun slips below the horizon hours before we reach the inn. Nearly twelve hours of hiking through the snow with only the briefest of breaks have made us a tragic sight. We drag ourselves up the path to the door, bedraggled and shivering, clustering together for warmth as Professor Walsh raps the knocker.

Melissa huddles next to me, her eyes fixed on the professor. I wind my hand around hers and she squeezes.

Tonight is the night. We'll get our proof, and Melissa can put this nightmare behind her.

First, though, every last one of us is sagging with weariness. Asher stands at his sister's back, reaching around her to stroke my arm. Lance is on my other side, stamping packed snow from his boots. And Annabelle and Thabo lean against each other, their breath fogging in the night air.

"About time." The owner of the inn yanks the door open and crosses her arms, blocking the threshold. "I nearly fed your suppers to the ponies."

"Then you saved yourself some cooking," Professor Walsh says, shouldering past her. The elderly woman staggers back against the door frame, her eyes wide and scandalized behind her glasses. Morgan murmurs an apology then steps inside, and we all squelch after.

This time, we're quick to kick off our boots. They're soaked through, icy cold, and blisters throb hot on my heels and toes the second the pressure leaves my feet.

The owner recovers her shock and pushes away from the door, marching to the key cupboard on the wall.

"You lost your rooms, of course." She smiles nastily at

154

Professor Walsh. "So you'll be cramming in together."

She gives us four keys total: one each for the professor and Morgan, then two rooms for the guys and girls. None of us complain; we're swaying on the spot, and besides, this inn has hot water. It's a damn paradise after that hike.

"Supper is in the breakfast room. Do not disturb the other guests."

I can't imagine what she thinks we're going to do; we each have dark shadows under our eyes, and we've barely spoken a word to each other in the last hour. Perhaps she's seen a few too many Hollywood films where American students wreck houses and do keg stands in the kitchen.

"Your suitcases are outside in storage." She clatters one final key down on a side table. "Good night."

Morgan takes one look at our faces then sighs, picking up the key.

"I'll bring the cases in. You all get warmed up."

No one argues. We trudge upstairs and find our rooms—twin beds with a makeshift cot in each. I go automatically to the cot, dropping my backpack with a groan. My shoulders pop as I stretch my arms overhead, my back muscles screaming.

"Are you still up for it, Gigi?" Melissa's voice is quiet. Annabelle glances between us, confused.

"Yes." I try to sound firmer than I feel. "I can do it."

The hot shower sluices some of my doubts away. The water pounds against the knots in my back, thawing out my numb fingers and toes, and I scrub away the layers of sweat and grime clinging to my skin. I linger a few extra selfish minutes, shampooing my hair twice and rubbing my scalp under the beating water.

One more push. One more nerve-wracking task, then I can fall into bed and we'll be one step closer to this all being over.

I try not to think about what happens after that. About the return to campus, and my silent dorm room, and going back to being Freaky Gigi. I haven't asked Lance or Asher what they want after this trip, and I won't today. There is a limit to my available courage in one night.

My stomach growls, the sound amplified by the bathroom tiles, and I crank the water off.

All right. I can do this.

* * *

I wait until after supper, when Professor Walsh is fed and happy. Our devices have charged for an hour, our rooms each a web of tangled cables, and Melissa dresses me in a pair of thick leggings and an off-the-shoulder sweater. Innocuous enough not to raise suspicion, but tempting enough to drive the professor to bad behavior.

We hope. There's a chance his offer a few days ago was meant to alarm me, and he wouldn't touch me with a ten foot pole.

"Don't be ridiculous," Melissa huffs, sweeping my hair over one shoulder. "You have three boyfriends, you idiot."

"Only two, actually." For now, at least. I pluck at the hem of the sweater.

"Oh, only two? My mistake. You're clearly repulsive."

I'm getting used to Melissa's sharp tone. Half the time her words are harsh and her voice is harsher, but there's a sparkle in her blue eyes. I've got the gnawing feeling that she was never as mean to me as I once thought.

Then again, when she makes me spin around in a full circle,

her mouth twists like I'm wearing a trash bag.

"Give her a break, Mel," Lance calls from one of the beds. "The man's a creep. He's not going to care what she's wearing."

He's sat with his legs bent and his arms braced on his knees, eyebrows lowered in a frown. Lance is not a fan of our plan, and neither is Asher, glowering beside him. They only agreed to it because we said we were doing it with or without them.

This way they'll be standing by. In case things get out of hand.

Annabelle and Thabo's voices float through the wall, laughing as they play cards. They excused themselves from this madness, and I don't blame them.

"All right. Final checks." Melissa tugs the phone from where it's lodged down the side of my bra. The red dot shines from the screen, with the timer showing it's recording.

I tuck the phone back away as Melissa checks my laptop, raising my eyebrows at the guys on my bed. Usually, Lance would leap at the chance to tease me for hiding shit in my bra. He's not laughing today. There's a muscle leaping in his jaw.

Asher stands up and crosses the room in three steps. He cradles my face, running his thumbs over my cheeks.

"Be careful. If you get scared even for a second, shout. We'll be right outside the door."

I nod, forcing my lips into a smile.

"I'm not worried," I lie.

He lowers his head and kisses me like we're the only people in the room. It's deep and lingering; a kiss which makes me tremble from the intimacy.

Lance is next. He shoulders Asher out of the way and tucks my hair behind my ear.

He sucks in a breath like he wants to say something, then

lets it out.

Nothing. Typical.

"You're a rock star, Gigi," he says at last. When he kisses me, I bite his lip and he groans.

"Save it for the creep." Melissa bundles my open laptop into my arms and ushers me to the door, ignoring Lance's glare.

"She's not going to *kiss* him."

"I'm not," I assure the room, then I'm stumbling out into the corridor. Professor Walsh is four doors down, around the corner. Morgan's room is right next door, and that adds steel to my spine as I raise my fist and knock.

"Come in," a low voice calls.

I take a deep breath, hitch my laptop up in my arms, and push the door open.

* * *

"Gigi." Professor Walsh seems surprised to find me in his doorway, his eyebrows climbing up his forehead. He leans back in the wooden chair at the room's narrow desk, his gaze flicking down the length of my body. He lingers on the bare skin of my shoulder and the way my leggings cling to my thighs.

I clear my throat and step into the room. The door closes with a snap.

Professor Walsh took the nicest room, of course—even with a queen sized bed, it's still more spacious than the tiny rooms the rest of us have crammed into. A bookshelf rests against the wall by the desk, the spines of the leather books adorned with Welsh titles in gold leaf. The professor's case sags open on the floorboards, dirty laundry spilling over the sides, and an expensive laptop whirs on the desk next to a sheaf of papers.

He eases his glasses off and tosses them on his keyboard. "What can I do for you?"

The usual irritation that sharpens his voice when he speaks to me is gone. Instead, his voice is low and honeyed, his mouth curling up on one side.

Has he forgotten what happened last night? How I found him cornering Melissa; how he threatened my grades for pulling her away?

"I thought you might come." Professor Walsh rubs his jaw. "You didn't like seeing me with another girl, did you, Gigi?"

"No, sir." That's true enough. The sight turned my stomach. I lift my laptop, spinning the screen so it's pointing at him. "I brought you the new outline for my submission."

Some of the professor's charm sloughs away, and he drops his hand with a harsh sigh. He jerks his chin, reaching for the laptop.

"Come on, then."

I don't pass it over. I walk around his outstretched hand and place the laptop carefully on the wooden desk, angling it for the best view of the room. His breath fogs over my neck, far too close, but I swallow and scroll to the top of my document. I have to lean over his lap, my thigh brushing his, but he doesn't move to give me space.

"I tweaked my thesis." A palm hovers over the back of my knee, not quite touching but close enough that the heat spreads over my skin. "I've come at the topic from a new angle, like you said."

The professor hums, not listening. A thumb rubs at the bottom of my thigh, and I fight down the urge to stomp on his foot. Sucking in a deep breath through my nose, I unstick my jaw and carry on.

"There are fewer primary sources this way, but I think I can compensate using this bibliography." I tap on the screen with my nail, tamping down a squeak when his palm flattens against my leg and slides up.

I want to run. Abandon my laptop here and sprint out into the mountains. But I haven't done what I came for yet; this is no good as proof. He hasn't said anything truly incriminating, and his hand is out of view of my webcam.

I straighten up and turn to face him. Lick my lips. His brown eyes track the movement.

"What are you doing?" I ask.

Professor Walsh smirks.

"Yes. I imagine this must be very new for you." His roaming hand slips under the hem of my sweater, grazing the bottom of my ass. I swivel slightly, trying get it on camera.

No luck. I clear my throat, forcing my muscles to relax, and let him pull me into his lap. I straddle his thighs, locking my knees around his hips and keeping my intimate areas far away from his groin.

My arms wind around his neck on autopilot. I toy with the ends of his hair.

"Do you do this with all your students?" I ask, feigning innocence.

He grabs my ass with both hands.

"Only the pretty ones."

That's some proof, definitely, but I need to make sure it's crystal clear. Inarguable. And it's like the professor read my mind, because he jerks me forward and grinds me against him. My head snaps back and I gasp out in genuine pain. He is not gentle.

"What if I don't want to?" My eyes slide to the laptop, and

the tiny lens of the camera.

He winds his fist in my hair and tugs my head back, scraping his teeth over my throat.

"Please. You came here of your own free will."

"Stop." I brace my hands against his chest and push. I've got what I came for, and now I need to get far away from this creep. "Get off me."

His arms cage me in tighter and I open my mouth to yell, but the bedroom door crashes open. Morgan surges into the room, yanking me out of the professor's lap by the back of my sweater, before slamming his fist into the older man's nose. There's a horrible crunching sound and blood spurts everywhere, and I fall back against the bookcase.

"Out. Now." Morgan holds the struggling professor down with one hand. The way he looks at me—I've never seen him so angry. His jaw is tight, and my stomach flips under his glare. I snatch my laptop off the desk and scurry out of the open door.

Chapter 12

A sea of arms grabs me when I stumble into the corridor. Melissa lifts the laptop out of my arms, squeezing my hand before she takes off around the corner. I blunder after her, made clumsy by the two full-grown men pawing at me.

"Will you get off?" I snap, shaking Asher off my arm. Lance lets go of my other shoulder, palms held up like I'm threatening them at gunpoint. I round on them both, safely around the corner from the professor's room, and they back up into the wall. "I'm fine. It was fine. We got what we needed. And Morgan burst in before I even had to call for help."

Lance mutters something about being right outside.

"Yes. You would have come in. I know that, you know that, the sheep outside know that. Now please shut up about it."

I'm being horribly rude, but I can't help it. The feeling of those arms caging me in, the fog of the professor's breath on my neck has jangled my nerves. Even though, rationally, I know nothing awful could have happened, I'm still raw with the sensation of being some kind of prey animal.

After all, I'm not over six feet tall like these guys. I don't have their broad shoulders or their dense, heavy bones. I'm just a relatively short girl with poor upper body strength who's half-blind without her glasses.

I suck in a shuddering breath, my stomach curdling, and wrap my arms around my waist.

"You guys go ahead." I can't meet their eyes. "I want a word with Morgan."

"We're not leaving you alone." Asher may have allowed me my rant, but his chin is set on this. He folds his arms. "You can come and wait in the room, or you can deal with us being out here."

Lance nods, glaring at me. Guess I'm pissing everyone off tonight. I sigh and sag against the wall, suddenly exhausted. The sleepless night with Melissa; the twelve hour hike in the snow; the shot of adrenaline when Professor Walsh touched my thigh. It all crashes down on me at once, sapping the strength from my limbs.

Wordlessly, Lance and Asher push off their wall and come to lean on either side of me. Together, the two of them prop me up, and I tip my head back against the whitewashed paint.

A grandfather clock ticks at the other end of the corridor, the pendulum swinging. I hold my breath, count to ten, then scrabble for both their hands. They wind their fingers through mine, both rubbing my knuckles. I wonder idly if they realize how similar they are. Like two halves of the same coin.

"Sorry." My voice is hoarse in the empty corridor. Asher nudges me with his shoulder, while Lance squeezes my fingers. It buoys me up, and a grin stretches over my cheeks. "I did it, though."

When I turn my head, Lance stares down at me, fierce pride etched over his face.

"We told you, Gigi. Rock star." I roll my eyes, desperately pleased.

163

I did it. I outsmarted the head of the department; I got us concrete proof of his abuse of power. A small, petty voice at the back of my mind grumbles about my future in the department; about my own grades and my hopes for that submission.

There's no way there won't be consequences for me. Whether outright or more covert.

It doesn't matter. I silence that nagging voice, turning to smile at Asher too. His blue eyes crinkle, his dimple appearing in his cheek, and warmth settles in my chest.

It was worth it. For Melissa. For all the other students Professor Walsh probably cornered in the past; for all the girls he might have preyed on in the future.

And for me.

Gigi Russell: rock star.

* * *

Morgan does not emerge from the professor's room for the best part of an hour. After a while, my jelly legs can't hold me up any longer, and the three of us slide down the wall into a heap on the floor. Our hands tangle together, my hair snags on both their shoulders, and still Asher and Lance wait with me.

The grandfather clock ticks. The pipes gurgle in the walls. Overhead, a floorboard creaks.

"What the fuck is he doing in there?" Lance finally asks, just as Morgan peels the door open. He steps quietly into the corridor, the door closing with a muffled snap, then walks the couple of feet to his own door.

"That's my cue." I clap Asher on the knee and, after two tries, push to my feet. Two sets of big hands boost me up, steadying me as I stand. I pat them both, smiling weakly at my helpers before I leave. My muscles are leaden as I round the corner, shuffling back along the floorboards.

Morgan turns to me, eyes wide, his grip fumbling on the door handle. He opens his mouth to speak, then glances at the professor's bedroom. Shutting his mouth with a click, Morgan pushes his door open and jerks his head inside.

I know it's nothing. A matter of practicality. But still my stomach flips as I cross over the threshold.

Morgan's room is smaller than the professor's, but neater too. His case stands upright in the corner of the room, his jacket hung on the hook. I drift towards the wooden chair by the desk, then veer at the last second towards the bed.

I'm not trying anything. But I'd rather not encourage my brain to relive the encounter by the desk next door.

Morgan doesn't speak immediately. He stands with his back to me, facing the door, apparently wrestling with some inner drama. Finally, he sighs, shoulders slumping, and turns the key in the lock.

Interesting.

He crosses to the desk, placing a warning finger over his lips. I nod, kicking my feet in the emptiness beneath his bed. Morgan levers his laptop open and starts a random playlist. What sounds like a movie soundtrack hums through the speakers, not loud enough to wake anyone but enough to muffle our words.

"What were you doing in there for so long?"

Morgan slides me a look before turning to lean against his desk.

"I could ask you the same thing."

"That's not a satisfactory answer."

"No, it's not."

I tilt my head up and count the cracks in the ceiling. Anything but this infuriating back and forth. After a moment, Morgan moves to the bedside and kneels at my feet, bracing his hands either side of me on the bed.

"Did he hurt you?" His expression twists. I swallow hard.

"No. I told you; we had a plan."

Morgan sighs and rocks back on his heels. Pulling his glasses off, he tosses them on the bed covers and rubs at his eyes. He must not be so cripplingly blind as I am without his glasses. Faker.

"Right. A plan."

He sounds so bitter. Morgan might be the king of self control, but I've never been great at tamping down impulses, so when the urge catches hold of me, I trace a fingertip along his eyebrow. It's soft. Arched. A thrill runs through me when he leans a fraction closer.

"I can't believe you did that, Gigi. It was such a huge fucking risk. I told you I would deal with it—"

"And I told you 'no, thank you.'"

I switch to his other eyebrow, then swoop down to follow the line of his cheekbone.

"If I hadn't come in—"

"Lance and Asher were right outside."

"They might not have heard you."

"And you might have burst in too early and ruined everything."

Morgan slams his mouth shut, pressing his lips together. He closes his eyes and pulls in a long breath through his nose, looking like I do when I need to count to ten.

I nudge him with my knee. "We got it. Video evidence."

166

Morgan nods without opening his eyes.

"Will you take over his position?"

Morgan snorts, finally looking at me.

"I'm a graduate student, not heir to the throne."

Right. That was dumb. I chew on the inside of my cheek and inspect my knees. There's a speck of fluff on my leggings. I pick it off, rolling it between my thumb and forefinger before wiping it on the bedspread.

A gentle hand tilts my chin up, and Morgan's stormy gray eyes burn into mine. He's touching me. Finally. I swallow, my mouth suddenly dry, as heat prickles over my skin.

Can he hear my pulse race? Surely he can. It's deafening, pounding in my ears, and there are no other sounds in the room except the soft music humming from his laptop.

I can't take it anymore. It's been two weeks of stolen glances; two weeks of waiting and longing. I snap.

Morgan's sweater bunches in my hands, my knuckles scraping against the hard planes of his chest. I seal my lips against his, our noses brushing, and for a horrible moment he's rigid. Unresponsive. I kiss him for a few seconds longer, just in case, then force myself to let him go. I flex my fingers, smoothing out the creases in his sweater, and sit back.

"I'm sorry. I shouldn't have done that. I—"

Morgan's mouth comes down on mine like the wrath of God. He kisses me hard, demanding, sliding his tongue past my lips and working my mouth until my jaw aches. Every touch we denied ourselves this trip, every kiss we didn't share—he makes up for it now, tenfold. I groan, dragging him off the floorboards and on top of me on the bed. He pushes me back against the threadbare pillows, slotting on top of me and grinding down.

It's perfect. It's everything I've been craving like an addict.

And then he rolls off me, horror etched on his face.

"Shit. Fuck. Gigi, I'm so sorry."

He goes to scramble off the bed, and I chase after him, gripping his shoulders. I slam him down against the wall, swinging a leg over his and straddling his lap.

"Stop." I give his shoulders a shake. "Stop a second." I close my eyes, reaching for my shreds of rational thought. They scattered the instant Morgan's lips met mine, and my brain has been blissfully empty since.

"Okay." I open my eyes and run a thumb along Morgan's lip. He's rigid underneath me, a tendon taut in his neck. "I want this. Do you want this? It's okay if not, you just have to say so."

"Of course I—" Morgan cuts off, glaring at the wall. "That's not the issue."

"After this trip, you won't be my tutor anymore."

"But we're still on this trip, Gigi. I can't touch you."

I hum and consider that for six seconds.

"All right," I say at last. "Can I touch you?" I trail a fingertip down the center of his chin and draw a line to the hollow of his throat. His voice box bobs as my finger passes over.

He doesn't say no.

Shifting my weight, I bypass the sweater. In an ideal world, I'd tear Morgan's clothes off like wrapping paper, but we're hovering on a knife edge as it is. Instead, I slide both palms down his chest, over his abdomen, and come to rest on his belt buckle.

"Please." I tap the metal with a fingernail. "I want to, Morgan."

Indecision wars in his eyes, his hands tightening on my hips. But finally he tilts his head back with a thud and whispers, "Okay."

The belt is harder to undo than I thought, my fingers clumsy, and I huff as I tug the end free. Heat blooms on my cheeks and I'm getting flustered, fumbling and embarrassed.

Morgan's hand rests on top of mine, stroking a thumb over the back of my hand. I nod, clear my throat, and settle myself. *It's not a test. It's something wonderful.*

Then I meet his eyes and pop his top button free.

I keep waiting for Morgan to stop me. To change his mind and push my hands away. But he leans back and watches me, gaze scorching, as I undo his clothes and pull out his cock.

He's hard as stone, the skin soft and warm. I give an experimental tug, and Morgan lets out a hiss.

"You're beautiful," I tell him, shuffling around until I'm knelt on the floor between his thighs. I keep my hand on him the whole time, circling my thumb around the head, and hopefully he knows that I'm referring to his whole person, not just the bit in my hand.

Morgan doesn't say anything, but he strokes a hand over my hair. He brushes my bangs out of my eyes, tucking a long strand behind my ear, then slides his palm to cup the base of my skull. I lean into his touch like a cat, humming when he scratches behind my ear.

Focus, Gigi. You won't get this chance again.

I press a kiss to the tip of his cock, absorbing his every expression. Morgan's eyes flutter. My chest feels so full, my heart swelling in my rib cage, but I don't tell him about that. I don't want to freak him out.

Instead, I suck him into my mouth, and give the most tender blow job of my life.

I've always envied people with a photographic memory. I figured it was like going through life on the easy setting. A test? No worries. Need to remember directions? Word for word. Forgot your card? Here are the precise payment details.

This would be the ultimate benefit, though, surely. Committing this exact moment to memory. I desperately try to absorb every detail: the little catches in Morgan's breath, the gentle tug of his grip in my hair, his salty taste. The size and weight of him on my tongue, and the delicious sensation of being filled. The way I grow slick and swollen between my legs at just the sight of him.

I draw it out as long as I dare, bringing him to the brink then backing off again, the rise and fall of his chest hypnotic. My lips are wet and pink and my hair mussed by the time I finally take pity on his tortured groans. I swallow him down, bobbing my head and pumping the base of his cock with my fist. Morgan curses, clenching two handfuls of bedspread, and barely gasps out a warning before he spills down my throat.

I work him through it all, swallowing it all down, and when I finally pull my mouth away with a wet pop, Morgan is slumped and boneless. I beam at him, wiping my mouth with my sleeve.

"I liked that." I lean over to kiss him, to let him taste himself on my lips. As my lips meet his, something shifts and falls out of my bra.

"Huh." I pull back and follow Morgan's stare to the phone in his lap. The screen is lit up, a giant red circle pulsing in the center as a timer counts the minutes. "Guess it's still recording."

Morgan jerks backwards, tucking his clothes back in place and staggering to his feet.

"It's okay!" I pause the recording and click off my phone, holding it up like a surrender. "We'll just cut it at the point I left Walsh's room. No one needs to know—"

"That two staff members hit on you?" Morgan sounds

disgusted, his voice rough with self-loathing. He paces to the far side of the room, scrubbing at his face.

I fumble to my feet and wait for him to turn around.

"Please, Gigi," he says to the wall. "Go back to your room."

I hover there for half a minute longer, until I can't bear the silence beneath the soft music. Tears blur my eyes, and I smooth my sweater into place before letting myself back into the corridor.

The door clicks shut, Morgan far behind it. My face crumples, and I rest my forehead on the wood.

I'm glad I don't have a photographic memory. I want to forget this night as soon as possible.

* * *

The minibus engine roars to life, our breathing already fogging the windows. I rest my forehead against the glass, the chill spreading through my skin, and watch the first blue wash of dawn tinge the mountain side. It's gloomy outside, frost crispy in the grass, and the buttery light in the inn windows mocks us.

I shiver, burrowing deeper into one of Lance's sweaters. It smells like him, especially around the neckline, and I stick my nose in the wool and inhale.

"The last couple weeks already feel like a dream," Asher murmurs next to me. I nod, my bangs sticking to the condensation on the window, and watch the pale blobs of sheep track through the heather.

I don't feel like talking.

We lurch forwards, the bus swaying on the uneven gravel driveway. The mountainside flows past outside the window,

171

coated with gorse and heather and dotted with trees. Tumble-down barns hold water troughs for livestock, or great mounds of chopped wood piled high. I watch it all slide past with a lump in my throat.

Like a dream.

I haven't asked Asher or Lance whether they want to continue this… arrangement back in college. My initial assumption was of course they wouldn't—there are beautiful, single people all over campus, and neither of them were exactly thrilled to share in the first place. But then Lance bundled me into his sweater this morning, teasing my hair out of the neckline, and when Asher slid into the seat next to mine on the minibus, he immediately checked my seat belt.

I am perfectly capable of taking care of myself. I can wrap up warm and adhere to road safety regulations. I'm a grown woman, after all, and—objectively speaking—a highly intelligent one.

Still. It's nice they care. It soothes the anxious churning in my stomach that's made me queasy since last night.

Keeping my eyes on the brightening landscape, I tug one mitten off with my teeth. Even crammed full of warm bodies, the minibus air is still frigid. Our breath fogs in front of our chins, eight miniature chimneys puffing at the carpeted roof. But I ignore the shock of cold air on my bare hand and slide it up Asher's sleeve.

The pulse in his wrist taps against the heel of my palm. I stroke my fingers through the soft hairs on his forearm.

One of the nice things about Asher is he never forces me to speak. He lets me anchor myself against his warm, muscled arm, and stare out of the window, mind drifting.

There are so many considerations. So many tasks lined up

waiting, now that we're returning home.

My incomplete submission.

Our final grades for the semester.

The choreographed downfall of our sleazy professor.

These thoughts and more jumble together in my brain, jostling for attention. I need to draft my next parental email. I need to discuss the future with my boyfriends. The succulent collection in my dorm room needs watering.

"What are you frowning at so hard, Gigi?" Lance calls.

I shrug, my breath fogging the glass. After a pause, Lance starts to talking to Melissa again, their conversation a hum in the background. Asher's muscles shift beneath my palm, then he slides his own hand into my sleeve.

His thumb skates back and forth over my wrist. I close my eyes and melt into the seat.

"It didn't go well with Morgan?" There's no triumph in Asher's voice. He sounds sad. I shake my head, pushing deeper into his sweater and gripping tight.

He kisses my temple, lingering with the cold tip of his nose in my hair.

"You still have us, Gigi."

* * *

I am not the ideal seatmate for a nervous plane passenger. When I get nervous, which I naturally do whenever I am launched into the sky in a tin can of recycled air, I calm myself down with fun facts.

For example: the air on planes was actually cleaner, with a higher oxygen content, when smoking was still allowed. The uncomfortable, sickly feeling that comes with traveling by plane is partly due to stingy oxygen levels and recycled air full of germs.

"Gigi, I love you, but please shut up."

I pat Melissa's hand where it clenches our shared arm rest. "That's fair."

I don't even voice my internal observations when our little trays of microwaved pasta arrive. Melissa pokes at her food with a plastic fork, turning over her penne like a farmer tilling the soil, then tosses her fork down without eating a bite and focuses on the bread roll.

A wise choice. I do the same.

"Everything is in place," she tells me for the hundredth time, cursing when her pat of butter won't spread. "We made multiple copies of both recordings, and they're ready to send to the board."

I cut the recording on my phone myself before handing it over to my collaborators. Not because I am ashamed of what happened with Morgan, but out of respect for his privacy.

Then I stomped off for a shower and refused to speak to anyone all night. It's a wonder they all still like me, really.

"This is going to work. It's got to. Right?" Melissa taps her orange juice cup against the tray, not looking at me. There's an excellent chance she's talking to herself, but I reply just in case.

"Yes. It's incontrovertible proof."

She nods, taking a bite of her roll. She chews for about four seconds before wrinkling her nose and tossing the stale bread onto the tray.

Agreed. Airplane food is an affront to taste buds everywhere.

Since I have Melissa trapped next to me for eight hours, I have plenty of time to build my courage. Finally, after watching a terrible kids' movie and our second read of the in-flight magazine, I force myself to ask the question that's been weighing on my tongue.

"Would you like to hang out? Back at college?" Melissa glances at me, her eyebrows shooting up, and heat blooms over my cheeks. Distantly, I hear myself rambling on. "We could get coffee. Or go to a bar. Maybe if we have similar courses, we could meet in the library—"

Mercifully, she interrupts me.

"For fuck's sake, Gigi. What did you think was going to happen?"

It's such an unhelpful answer that I forget to be embarrassed for a second.

"Oh, come on. That could mean literally anything. Answer the question: do you want to hang out or not?"

It's not how the advice columns recommend making a friend, but it's done now. I can't take it back. Melissa rolls her eyes.

"It's sweet that you thought you had a choice in the matter. We're friends. Get over it."

It takes a minute for her words to sink in, but then I beam at the grumpy girl hogging our armrest. She holds up a palm, eyes narrowed.

"I have some ground rules, though. For as long as you're dating my brother, I never want details about your sex life."

I draw a cross over my chest. I have Annabelle for that, anyway.

"What about Lance?"

Melissa shudders. "That's just as bad."

I nod, and it's settled. Friends.

I suck in a deep breath of recycled air.

Chapter 13

A week later, Melissa slams her laptop shut on my desk. "This is bullshit. *Bullshit.* How can they possibly sweep this under the rug?"

She spins around, hands clenched in her hair, and begins to pace. My dorm room is cramped at the best of times, but with Lance sprawled on the bed and Asher leaning against the bookcase, she can only manage a few good strides in each direction. I draw my feet up onto the desk chair, crossing my legs.

"I suppose it's not unusual for college boards to ignore complaints of sexual harassment."

Lance grunts, his face harsh as he stares out my window. It's dark outside, silver threads of rain glinting against the night sky.

One eye on Melissa, I lever her laptop back open and skim the email a second time. *We appreciate your concern... very serious allegations... a respected and trusted member of faculty.*

No suspension. No internal investigation. No outreach for affected students. I draw my phone out of my jeans pocket and check the email icon. It's me in the video, after all—my body the professor was pawing at.

Nothing. Not a word.

Only a thinly veiled warning not to release the recordings. We study here with the blessing of the board, after all.

Rage floods through me, hot and unexpected. I used to get like this as a child, be rendered speechless by flashes of white-hot fury, but years of anger management and coping techniques helped to regulate my emotions.

This, though. I could burn down this whole campus, with those self-righteous board members locked inside.

"No." I toss my phone onto the desk with a clatter. Asher cocks his head, watching me. "I'm not done. I don't give a shit what they do."

Melissa huffs, marching to my side. She leans over my shoulder, rereading the email, her knuckles white where she clutches the desk. The wood creaks, and she straightens, absentmindedly twirling my ponytail round her finger.

"What's the plan?"

I smirk up at her, violence rushing through my veins.

"We spread the word."

* * *

I shift on the stone wall, my boots scraping where I sit cross-legged, and my notebook slides off my lap and lands in a puddle on the sidewalk. It floats among the flecks of dirt, spine up and pages splayed.

Two weeks' worth of notes. Ideas for assignments. The first draft of my next email to my parents. I purse my lips and watch the notebook drift, but I can't bring myself to really care.

Not today. Not on this excellent, triumphant day.

"Want me to get that?" Asher hops off the wall next to me and crouches beside the puddle. He plucks my notebook out

177

of the grimy water, wrinkling his nose as he lays it out next to my backpack.

I may not care about the fate of my notebook, but I do care about Asher. I lean down and stroke his long blond hair, running my fingers through the strands. He grins up at me, eyes twinkling, the same vicious joy flushing his cheeks as mine.

It's been a long couple of weeks. Endless nights of phone calls and video chats, of in-person meetings at every local newspaper office within fifty miles. I'm not one for social media—I can barely navigate conversations off-screen—but Melissa assures me that our recordings have spread far and wide.

It's appropriate for Professor Walsh to go viral. The man is a disease.

A camera crew hurries past, stomping in the puddle as they go and splattering Asher with muddy water. He grumbles and stands up, brushing down his pants as Lance howls with laughter on my other side. I elbow Lance hard in the ribs, but all he does is keep laughing and offer me popcorn from the bag he's snacking on.

Popcorn. Honestly. To watch a man's downfall. Lance has a weird sense of humor.

The news crews cluster around the History building, their vans parked haphazardly over the quad. It's mid-morning, and students stream around the crews and their cables, rolling their eyes and huffing as they try to get to class.

It's old news here. The Llewellyn College board has reluctantly spoken.

Professor Walsh is out.

This probably could have been a quieter affair. The professor could have boxed up his office and quietly slipped off campus, the rest of the world none-the-wiser.

It was an option. But a certain inside source in the History department informed us of Professor Walsh's allocated time to collect his things. And, well, it seemed selfish to hold on to a detail like that.

"That's him," Melissa says from Asher's other side, a cruel smile curling her lips. She kicks her heels against the wall with undisguised glee as the professor exits the History building, only to be swamped by news crews.

It's hard to tell from across the street, but he looks like he's aged a decade over the last two weeks. His hair is unkempt, his jaw dark with stubble, and his shirt is creased and untucked. He gestures angrily at the reporters, the box of his belongings wobbling in his arms, the din swallowing whatever he's saying.

It's a beautiful start to the new semester.

Lance offers me the bag again, and I grab a handful of popcorn. It's sweet and salty, just like Lance, and I frown at the chaos over the street as I chew.

I don't want to miss a *second* of this.

The news crews surround Professor Walsh, blocking our view, but I can't get too frustrated with them. They're our insurance—the reason the board can't kick us out for releasing those recordings. They're already facing uncomfortable questions from parents and donors about why they suppressed our complaint.

Good. There are so many intelligent people in the world who would thrive in positions of leadership. Why should a bunch of crusty old men coast by completely unchallenged?

It's over too soon. I could cheerfully have watched a three hour extended director's cut of Professor Walsh's public humiliation. But after ten minutes of arguing with the reporters, he elbows his way through the crowd and marches to his car parked nearby on the street. The camera crews trail him, microphones bobbing in his face, but he slams his car door and peels away down the street. His tires squeal as he weaves over the road, but he doesn't even crash.

Too bad. That would have made for great morning television.

We watch until he's out of sight, then sit a while longer as the news crews pack up. A few of them film summaries, polished reporters in tailored suits speaking in front of the History building. Then they load up their vans, too.

The last of the crews pulls out of the quad, and we sit in silence on the wall.

"It's kind of an anti-climax." Asher glances at his sister. "Did we do enough? Should we do more?"

Melissa sighs happily and hops off the wall, stretching her arms until her shoulders pop. Her berry-red coat matches her lipstick. She's a woman dressed to kill.

"It was perfect. He looked miserable."

Some of the tension bleeds out of Asher.

"He is miserable," a voice calls. "You nailed him to the wall."

Morgan stands a few feet down the sidewalk, his hands in his pockets. He's smart in a dark coat and collared shirt—he must be teaching today—and his dark hair shifts in the breeze. My eyes rake over every inch of him, my pulse thudding in my ears.

"Congratulations." Morgan steps closer. "You won."

I say nothing—my mouth won't work—but the others cover for me. They thank him and chat, laughing about the morning's theatrics, and I'm free to sit here and stare.

It's been a long two weeks for a lot of reasons.

I thought it would get easier: that we'd come back, and without all that intense proximity, my feelings would fade. I'd move on with Lance and Asher—I can hardly complain that I'm lonely—and Morgan would become an old crush.

But the second I lay eyes on him again, it crashes over me like a wave. I twitch towards him; I forget how to breathe; all the sounds of the street fade away. I don't even notice the others have left until Morgan sits next to me on the wall and we're alone.

"I'm proud of you, Gigi."

I unstick my tongue from the roof of my mouth.

"Thank you," I rasp. "Me too."

He's so close that when the breeze ruffles his hair, I catch the scent of his shampoo. I lean closer, chasing the smell of citrus.

For once, Morgan doesn't lean back.

"I read your submission."

"Oh." I didn't send it to him. But I left it with the department secretary to mail.

"It's incredible work, Gigi."

I let out a breath, and for the first time since Morgan arrived, a smile creeps over my face.

"You think so?"

"Definitely. All those professors and graduate students won't know what hit them."

I nod, suddenly shy, and pluck at a loose thread on my jeans. Out of the corner of my eye, Morgan inches closer until his leg is mere inches from mine.

"What is it?"

I address the loose thread, smoothing it between my fingers.

"I miss you."

For a long stretch of time, Morgan says nothing. There's only the rumble of traffic passing on the street, and the distant hum of conversation on the quad.

Then, quietly: "I miss you too."

He pushes upright and strides away, his shoulders tense under his jacket.

* * *

"Pizza or Chinese?"

Lance bends down to read the menus on the fridge. I hop up onto the kitchen counter, reveling in all the *space*. Lance and Asher's apartment is huge compared to my grotty little dorm room, and where there are dried ramen noodles and empty hot sauce containers on the counters in my shared kitchen, here there is a mug stand and an honest-to-God fruit bowl. I pick out an orange, turning it in my hands and raise it to sniff at the peel.

Seriously. I'd date these guys if they lived in grimy dorms, same as me, but this apartment is one hell of a perk.

Asher wanders into the kitchen and sets the coffee maker running. This is a new tidbit I've learned about Asher: he cannot function without caffeine. Even when he drags himself out of bed before dawn to drive twenty minutes to the coast and hit the waves, he gets up ten minutes earlier so he can brew himself some jet fuel coffee. I watch him dig out mugs and creamer, a fond smile tugging my lips.

"Gigi?" Lance glances over his shoulder, waving a hand at the menus.

I shrug. "I don't care. They're all equally unhealthy."

Lance rolls his eyes but plucks a Chinese menu off the fridge and slaps it onto my lap.

"Choose your poison."

I kick my ankles around him, caging him in with me.

"Sir, yes, sir."

Lance's eyes heat, and the menu slithers to the counter forgotten, but a knock at the door sends us springing apart. I raise my eyebrows at Lance, but he says nothing, patting my knee and clapping Asher on the shoulder as he leaves.

The door opens and low voices sound in the hall. I pick up the menu and flick to the noodles.

A throat clears, and it's ridiculous, but I recognize that sound. My head jerks up, and I stare at Morgan in the kitchen doorway.

There's no formal coat or button-down shirt tonight. He looks like any other graduate student—rumpled and tired, clad in a sweater and jeans. His glasses are missing, and it makes him look younger, while his hair sticks up on one side like he's been running his hands through it.

Morgan holds his palms up in front of him.

"I know I'm intruding—"

"You're here," I breathe. Lance and Asher share knowing looks, but I ignore them both, sliding down off the counter. I wasn't expecting to see anyone else tonight, and I'm dressed in thick socks, a pair of leggings, and one of Asher's old t-shirts.

I want to leap on him—fling my arms around his neck—but this visit could mean anything. So I hang back, the edge of the counter digging into my spine, and wait for Morgan to talk.

"I, uh." He clears his throat. "I changed my teaching assignments."

It's a blow. Since coming back from the trip, Morgan teaching one of my classes was my last excuse to see him.

"Right." I twist the t-shirt hem in my hands. "That's… good?"

"I hope so." Morgan steps forward. "I'm not teaching you anymore."

I grimace, looking down at my feet. One of my socks has bunched at the ankle.

"Gigi." Morgan's shoes stop an inch from my toes. He tips up my chin. "Do you understand what this means? We can *do* this. If you'll still have me."

Moisture wells in my eyes, and I fist my hands in his sweater, but I pause. Lance and Asher stand on either side of Morgan, watching me carefully.

"Is this okay?" I croak, looking between them. Lance smirks as Asher nods, face solemn.

"We invited him for a reason, Gigi."

I let out a frankly embarrassing sound and bury my face in Morgan's chest. His arms come around me, holding me tight, and if I could seal us together into one organism, I would.

"Don't crush the poor man," Lance says, but his fingers play in my hair. Asher runs a fingertip down my squished cheek. "Morgan: pizza or Chinese?"

Morgan shrugs, his sweater shifting under my face.

"Either. They're both delicious and terrible."

Lance groans, and I grin into the scratchy wool over Morgan's chest. He should know by now that I'm always right.

* * *

We eat first, cramming onto the sofa to watch *Shark v. Rhino* or some other incomprehensible B-movie. I glue myself to Morgan's side, staring after him every time he gets up to grab a drink or slip away to the bathroom.

"He's not going anywhere," Asher says when Morgan goes to fetch a beer. "Try and relax." He pulls my socked foot into his lap and kneads at the arch, and I burrow down into the sofa cushions.

"It really doesn't bother you?" I whisper, my words swallowed up by the screams in the movie.

Asher shakes his head, and Lance gives me a sinful smirk.

"Far from it." He leans in, presses a kiss to my throat, then nips at my earlobe. "I want to see you take all three of us, Gigi."

I shiver, suddenly overheating, but before I can suggest opening a window, Morgan comes to stand right in front of me.

"This movie is awful." He turns and clicks the remote. The screams fade and the screen dims to black. "Gigi." Morgan leans down and braces a hand on either side of my head. "I'm dying. Please tell me you want this."

I nod. Asher rubs harder at my foot, and Lance shifts closer. Morgan runs his thumb over my bottom lip, frowning as he does it.

"I messed this up every step of the way, but I'll make it up to you. I promise."

I slide my palms up his neck and tug him closer.

"I don't care about that."

I really don't. Especially when his lips meet mine, and I moan into his mouth. Lance curses softly next to me, and Asher skates a palm up my calf.

This is real. This is happening. If I don't catch fire first.

I surge up off the sofa, wrenching my leg off Asher's lap, and spin Morgan around before slamming him down in my place. All three of them gaze up at me, eyes heated and cheeks flushed.

"Take your shirts off." My voice cracks, but they hurry to it, yanking their clothes over their heads.

Three bare chests greet me: all mouthwatering yet unique. Lance is the bulkiest, sparse brown hair trailing down to his abdomen. Asher is leaner, his pale skin smooth, but toned from hours on a surfboard. And Morgan is somewhere between the two, his muscles a delicious surprise.

Who knew you could build a chest like that from heaving around stacks of books?

"Undo your pants." My voice is stronger this time. Surer. How many times have I daydreamed about this moment? I know exactly what to say. They each unbutton their jeans, shifting to slide them a few inches down their hips.

I gnaw on my bottom lip, soaking in the sight in front of me. I'm so flushed, I could heat this whole apartment complex. When I shift my weight between my feet, my clit throbs in my panties.

"Touch yourselves," I rasp. "I want to watch."

Lance smirks at me, smug as ever as he tugs his cock from his underwear. He's already hard—all three of them are—and even though I've seen them all before, it still makes me squirm. I press my thighs together, desperate to touch myself too, but I cross my arms over my chest instead.

I've waited weeks for this. I can wait a few minutes longer.

They work their cocks slowly. Teasing me. I growl, but I stay rooted to the spot.

"Tell me what you want," I order.

It's Morgan that speaks up, circling the tip of his cock with his thumb.

"Just you, Gigi. Any way that you'll have us."

The others nod. And maybe I'm weak, but I can't put it off

any longer. I wrench Asher's t-shirt over my head, kick my leggings off, and clamber into Morgan's lap. He grips my waist, rocking up against me, and Asher reaches between us to tug my panties to the side.

"Condom," Morgan grits out. Lance tears open a packet and rolls it onto Morgan's cock with a steady hand.

Morgan barely notices. He palms my breast, rolling my nipple between his fingers.

"So perfect," he breathes, then I sink down on his length and his forehead drops to my shoulder. It's a stretch, but I'm so wet already that he glides straight inside.

"Fuck." Asher flips my hair off one shoulder.

"Yeah." Lance spanks my ass. The sting shocks me into moving, and I rock on Morgan's lap, groaning at the delicious friction. He fills me up, pressing against every inch of me, my clit catching against him with each thrust.

"Come closer," I gasp. They don't need telling twice. Asher and Lance squeeze in tight where I can reach. I grip a cock in each hand and pump them as I ride Morgan's lap. He bites his lip, his eyes darting between my hands on the others and the place where we're joined.

I suck that lip between my teeth and bite down.

Morgan groans, then reaches between us to work my clit. He rubs tight, steady circles, winding me tighter until I can't take it anymore. I slam down on his cock, bury my face in his neck, and fall apart with a cry.

Dimly, I feel Asher and Lance tense up, curling forward, then they spill over my hands. Morgan swells inside me, gripping my hips like a vice as he comes. I keep my face tucked away, catching my breath, then wipe my fingers against Lance and Asher's stomachs before I sit up.

Three dazed faces stare back at me, their cheeks flushed and their pupils blown wide.

Yeah. A smug grin tugs at my lips, and I flick Lance's nipple. This is good.

* * *

"This is nuts." Lance tugs at the collar of his wet suit, grimacing when it smacks back against his skin. "It's fucking February. We should all be certified."

"Never took you for a little bitch, Lockford." Melissa smirks, tying her hair in a ponytail. Lance lunges for her, and they stagger across the sand, wrestling upright, the noise of their bickering swallowed up by the waves.

A hand winds through mine, and I smile up at Morgan. It's icy cold, the wind whistling straight through our wet suits, and it's so early the sky is tinged pink. Steel gray waves crash against the shore, foaming and rabid. We left our warm bed for this.

I don't mind. None of us do, really, even though none of us except Asher are great surfers.

It's worth the yawns and the sting of icy sea water to see Asher's dimple come out.

"All right. I'll take you guys one at a time so I can keep an eye on the currents." The man of the hour tucks his surfboard under one arm and grins at me. "Gigi? Feeling brave?"

He belongs here. His hair dances in the breeze, the same color as the sand. My stomach swoops and I blush under his gaze, even after months together.

"Sure." I squeeze Morgan's hand before I let go. "Always."

It's a lie when it comes to surfing. The last time we came

here before class, I nearly fell off and face-planted a jellyfish. Every time something brushes against me under the water, my throat clenches tight and I bite back a scream.

I want to do it, though. I want to be brave. And besides, I bragged about surfing in my last email to my parents. I bragged about other things, too, but it's the surfing they asked me about.

I chew on the inside of my cheek as we stride across the sand, my shoulder knocking against Asher's bicep. Parents are weird. They want to hear about grades, and extra-curriculars, but you tell them you're dating a staff member and they don't reply for two straight emails. And when they *do* finally start writing again, they skate over it like you never said anything.

I haven't even mentioned Lance and Asher yet.

Gotta save something for Easter vacation.

Author's Note

Thank you for reading Gigi's story! It was a challenge to write, but I firmly believe that EVERYONE deserves to be represented in romance. Gigi may not be neurotypical, but she is passionate, smart, caring and brave. Who better to have her own harem?

If you enjoyed Gigi's story, please consider leaving a review! Reviews help readers to find lesser-known books and authors, and writing one officially makes you a Wonderful Person.

Finally, in the undying words of Keanu Reeves: Be excellent to each other.

Let's keep in touch!

If you enjoy my work and you want to be the first to know what I'm up to, please consider signing up for my newsletter! I send bonus content, book recommendations, cover reveals, and other goodies twice a month.

Subscribers also get a free download of my *Lords of Summer* prequel: *Before the Fall.*
   Here's a sneak peek...

* * *

She's here.
   She's arrived in the quad.
   Layla Mackenzie.
   I glance up between the curtain of my dark hair, my elbows resting on my knees. It's still early September, barely the start of second year, and summer hasn't relinquished its hold. The air is warm—warm enough that the students dotted around the grass and on the benches are still in t-shirts. They kick back, legs stretched out, laughing in groups or studying solo.
   It's the beginning of the year, and everything feels heavy with promise. With potential.
   Layla picks her way across the grass, stepping over out-stretched legs and winding between abandoned backpacks.

She nods at a few of the groups; waves at a couple of solo students. They wave back, calling out her name, inviting her to join them.

Everyone loves Layla. What's not to love? The buttery sunshine dances over her, drawing deep bronze highlights out of her dark red hair.

Fuck.

No one makes an ass of me like Layla. I look at her creamy skin, her sweet, cheeky smile, and all words dry up in my throat. The only thing that hurts worse than looking at her is not looking at her, and every second in her presence is a sweet torture. And all the while that I'm here dying, she has no clue. She probably doesn't even know my name.

It doesn't matter. She's too good, too happy for me to let myself get near. I'm not built for sweet girls, nor for holding hands on the way to class. No gentle kisses in the sunshine. No: if I got my callused hands on her, she'd come away stained.

I couldn't bear that.

As if she can hear my thoughts, Layla glances in the direction of my bench, and I drop my gaze to my hands. I run a thumb over the opposite knuckle, back and forth, feigning interest in the scars flecking my skin.

It was a rough summer back home. It always is. Rough, but satisfying: endless days of back-breaking labor, sweetened by the jokes between workers, and at the end of the season, the tangible results. Our family ranch was built on sweat and blood, started from the ground up. It's bigger now, one of the most successful in the state, but the demands are bigger too.

The blood and sweat never go away; it's a yearly tithe, and we pay it.

I risk a glance at Layla again, to see which lucky bastards she decided to sit with, but she's gone from the center of the quad. My head jerks up fully, and I whip my gaze around, only to find her sat a few feet away on the next bench over.

My heart speeds in my chest, hammering against my rib cage, and my mouth goes dry.

Fuck. This is the problem: this is what she does to me.

She makes me foolish, reckless. Raw.

Layla sees me looking around like I've lost my puppy, because of course she does - she's not blind. I lose sight of her for fifteen seconds and the panic practically bleeds from my pores. She's not the only one who notices either; the nearest group lazing on the grass are watching me curiously too.

I let my eyes meet hers for a split second, then slide my gaze away, like I'm still looking. Like I haven't found who I'm searching for.

I swear she deflates just a little.

Fuck. I want to go over there, to just snatch up my stuff and march over to sit beside her. I want to snuff out any doubt in her mind that she's the one I'm looking for—she's always the one.

Every day, I come to the quad during lunch for the sole purpose of seeing her. I sit on this bench, or lay out on the grass—that part isn't important. What's important is that she always comes too, usually alone. And she always seems to pick out a spot near me to sit.

I don't kid myself that she does it on purpose. We've barely said ten words to each other, even since Eli started bringing her to hang out with our group. But maybe—subconsciously—she's as drawn to me as I am to her. Maybe she feels the same pull, the same fishing hook in her gut tugging her towards me.

The only relief is when she's near. Then I can breathe again. God, I sound fucking insane.

See, this is why I can't bother the girl. If I say any of this shit out loud, if I tell her how she makes me feel, I'll be locked away in a padded room and they'll be right to do it.

Better to enjoy these stolen moments with her, then force myself back to my day.

It's not like I can tell the others, either. Eli, Jasper and Nate. I've seen the way they look at her too. We're all as fucking bad as each other.

Jealousy curls through me, hot and vicious, whenever any of my friends talk to her. And though they've never acknowledged it, they seek her out almost as much as I do. At least once a week, I'll see Jasper stood behind her in line at the campus coffee shop, leaning down with a smile curling his lips to murmur in her ear. His wavy blond hair slides forward, tickling at her cheek.

I see the shiver that runs up her spine, too. It makes me want to tear him away from her, to throw him through the huge glass window.

But when he catches up with me a few minutes later, coffee in hand, I always force a smile. What am I going to say, anyway? Hey, man, that's my dream woman that I never plan to speak to?

Nate and Eli are just as bad. Nate gets this feral glint in his eye whenever she's near, like he's putting out pheromones or some shit. A lot of girls are scared of Nate, with his buzzed head and the tattoos all over his arms and chest. But he makes Layla laugh with his savage words, the sound ringing bright between the pale stone buildings.

I long for the sound of her laugh even as I hate that I'm not the one to draw it from her.

Eli is the worst of all. He spoke to her first, got to know her in some tutorial group, so he thinks he has some kind of claim on her. It makes me want to fucking scream when he tucks an arm around her shoulders, possessive and sure.

I saw her first. I fucking craved her first.

I just never did anything about it.

Eli and Jasper round the corner to the quad, moving with confident strides. They laugh and talk as they walk, raising a hand each when they notice me. We found each other during orientation week of first year, Nate included. It was so fucking easy, like four jigsaw pieces slotting into place.

I've never had that before. Not with friends, and certainly not with family. What we have, the four of us—it's like breathing. Unconscious and vital.

Both of their eyes light up when they notice Layla on the next bench over. I have to remind myself then that these guys are brothers to me —that I can't lose my shit over a dumb surge of jealousy.

Then Eli strides straight past my bench to sit next to Layla. A dark curl falls over his forehead, and his eyes crinkle when he speaks.

No. No, he can't tuck her hair behind her ear—can't make her blush like that. I shoot a glance at Jasper to see what he thinks, but he's watching the two of them with heat in his gaze. I want to shake him, then rip Eli away from Layla and shake him too. Can't they see how wrong this is?

It should be me on that fucking bench.

I tried to stay away for so long. Since the first time I saw Layla, way back in October of first year. I thought I could protect us both by keeping away, but now she's everywhere I look, and my friends have set their sights on her.

Fuck that. I won't bow out without a fight.

Today is the day I tell Layla Mackenzie how I feel.

Teaser: Spring Kings

They shut me away for my safety.

They should have triple checked the lock.

My bodyguard Jamie is my shadow. He escorts me everywhere; he plans my days.

He's so damn beautiful that maybe I wouldn't mind, except this has already gone on too long.

There's a whole city out there. A world to explore. Music, laughter, *life.*

That's why I do it: dive out of the car and disappear into the crowd. Why I spend my stolen hours with a gorgeous musician and the captain of a riverboat.

Jamie's always so serious. Well, it's time to play a game.

Count to ten, Jamie. Then come find me—if you can.

Spring Kings is a standalone contemporary reverse harem novel. It contains explicit language, high heat, and a guaranteed HEA.

Available now on Amazon.

Read on for a sneak peek…

* * *

I dunk the nail polish brush in the glass bottle, swirling it around before drawing it back out. Two more careful strokes and the toes on my right foot are finished: wet and shining under the lantern's glow. Emerald green. I blow my hair out of my face and shift on the bench, drawing up my ruined leg.

It's stiff. Scarred. Warped. And it's going to have pretty green toes, damn it.

A breeze drifts through the shadowed gardens, wafting the scent of jasmine over my cheeks. I tip my head back, eyes closed and nail polish forgotten just for a second.

That breeze. After another long, muggy day, with air so hot and heavy you can chew on it—that breeze feels so good it should be illegal. I lift my elbows, holding up my arms so the cool air can reach all the sticky bits.

"Emerald glitter?" I squint one eye open and find our head of security, Jamie, leaning against a statue of a lion. Jamie wears a suit while the lion is dressed in white stone, but they each have matching manes. "What's the occasion?"

I squeeze my eye shut again and go back to ignoring him. Jamie's always somewhere close. Watching. Keeping an eye. Usually I like having him near—like having someone to chat to—but right now my leggings are rolled up on my scars and I'd give anything for him to turn around and sidle back round the ponds.

"Francesca?"

I huff. He knows I hate my full name.

"Doctor's appointment."

Which Jamie knows, because he's in charge of my schedule. Dad has him run this estate like a fine-tuned Swiss clock, all-knowing and all-seeing. And tomorrow, for my appointment, it'll be Jamie driving me into the city.

He hums and pushes off the lion, strolling closer with his hands tucked in his suit pockets. He always dresses flash, just like the rest of Dad's men, but sometimes when he lifts his arm I glimpse the gun holstered under his jacket.

It's kind of funny. I can't picture Jamie ever firing it. To me, he's the man who sits up playing cards on the deck when I can't sleep. Who sneaks me beignets from the best bakery in the French Quarter, and spent nearly twenty minutes scooping out a moth that fell in the fountain.

"It'll be right."

Jamie sounds like Dad when he talks like that, but I don't tell him so. I let him crouch in front of my garden bench and inspect my toes.

While he's looking at the emerald glitter, I inch my injured leg back down to the floor.

"Oh, no you don't."

A warm hand wraps around my ankle and places my heel back on the bench. His grip is firm but not harsh, and he holds me there, the pad of his thumb rubbing back and forth over a scar.

I hold my breath, but it's like he doesn't even realize what he's doing to me. Jamie plucks the brush out of my grip and dips it in the polish, swirling it around.

"Are you worried? About tomorrow?"

A line creases Jamie's forehead as he paints my big toe, slow

199

and careful.

"No." It's true, mostly. I've had a thousand of these appointments. The doctors are just going through the motions at this point, too scared to tell Dad he's fussing over nothing.

I can't blame them. Dad can be fierce, especially when his protective instincts are triggered. And when it comes to my leg, Dad is all instinct. He's just so damn guilty.

"Then why are you sulking out here on your own?"

I level Jamie a glare, but he smirks at my second toe. If he weren't engaged in such a delicate task, I'd thump him on the shoulder.

"Maybe I want to make your job harder. You've had an easy ride of it so far, don't you think? Keeping an eye on the estate and babysitting little ol' me."

"Is that all you think I do?" Jamie asks mildly.

I flick a lock of his red hair, tickling at his collar. "Yup. It's like you retired at thirty-five."

"Thirty-two." He sounds strained.

"Well, I'm just saying. It could be good for you. Sharpening those skills. Like when office workers go on courses about spreadsheets."

Jamie sighs and looks up then, his blue eyes pinning me to the spot. Back and forth, his thumb rubs over my scar. Back and forth.

Goosebumps prickle over my bare arms, never mind the warm night.

"You can hide if you like." His mouth quirks up on one side. "But you know I'll always find you."

Promises, promises. Dad would have Jamie's hide if he heard him say things like that.

Sure enough, footsteps crunch down the gravel path, summoned by our flirting. Jamie pushes the nail polish brush into my hand and straightens. He's upright and out of reach by the time the footsteps round the fountain.

"Carrick." Jamie nods respectfully.

Me? I poke my tongue out at Dad. He strolls over, his eyes flicking between us, measuring the distance. I'm half surprised he doesn't whip out a measuring tape and make us each hold an end.

Dad is like Jamie: sharp suits and sharp smiles. But older. Harsher. With graying hair and great shadows under his eyes, and plenty of bite along with his bark.

"Behaving yourself?" He ruffles my hair and I nod, though I'm not sure who he's talking to.

"Always."

He snorts. "Now if that were true."

Then what? The question bubbles up in my mouth, but I choke it back. It's not like I'm difficult or unruly. I do my lessons; I get good grades. I'm set to graduate early from distance learning with Llewellyn College next month.

And then what? Really: then what? I've barely left this estate in the last eight years. My big outing is to the doctor each month.

I don't know what I could do to behave better. To earn more trust. Hell, I haven't even jumped Jamie's bones, and the thought crosses my mind at least twice a day.

I can't live the rest of my life in my parents' estate. The damn Siamese cats have more freedom. But every time I bring up looking for jobs, or even taking on a role in Dad's business, it's like I pulled open his shirt and stabbed him straight in the heart.

Not today. I can't have that same argument again. Not with

the appointment tomorrow. That reminds me—I dip the nail polish brush back in the bottle and set to painting my last two toes.

"You after your doctor?" Dad eyes my sparkly nails, and I wiggle them. The flecks of glitter catch the lantern light.

"Hardly. He's about a hundred years old."

"Then what's with the fancy feet?"

I shrug. "Distraction tactics."

Dad and Jamie both fall quiet, and I tug my leggings down until they cover my scars. I shouldn't have said that. He already feels guilty enough.

The silence stretches for a moment before he speaks again, and I see Jamie shifting out of the corner of my eye. Jamie's nearly as protective of Dad as he is of me. If Dad weren't such a scary bastard, I bet Jamie would follow him around and paint his toes too.

Loyalty. That's what Carrick O'Brien inspires in his men. Loyalty and a healthy dose of fear.

It's weird for me to picture—like trying to imagine Jamie firing his gun. To me, Dad's a pussycat. He sits down next to me on the bench and rests his elbows on his knees.

The sigh that comes out of him rattles on for half a year.

"You should take a day off."

He hangs his head, rolling his shoulders. This is privileged viewing—none but family and Jamie get to see Dad like this.

Tired. Old. Aching after a long day.

"Soon, Frankie. I promise. But we've got business to attend to first."

This is not news. The O'Brien family always has business to attend to. It's what I keep trying to wriggle into, offering to shadow workers or intern or do *anything*, just to get involved.

Dad won't have it. He says I'm too pure for the family work. I say that's sexist bull.

"More meetings?" I ask, because he's tired and I won't kick him while he's down. Dad nods his head, still hanging.

"A whole week of them on the west coast."

Huh. That is new. Our business is usually area-specific. We've got our claws in this city, and in deep, but that's that.

"When do you leave?"

"Tomorrow. Your mom and I will see you off to the doctor, then head straight to the airport."

For a crazy moment, panic claws at my throat. The thought of being stuck here alone, of being left behind—I can barely breathe.

But Dad pats the back of my hand, and it brings me back to earth. They're not ditching me; they're working. Flying for hours to meet with boring business people, then flying back to make big, dull decisions.

I swallow hard. "I'll miss you."

Dad turns and gathers me into his arms, all misty eyed.

"Oh, Frankie girl. We'll miss you too."

Over Dad's shoulder, Jamie watches us both, leaning against the stone lion. It's dark in the gardens, the sky inky black, and the lantern light bounces off his eyes.

It's been a long time since we were left here alone.

I shiver and hug Dad harder.

* * *

The suitcases are packed and ready when I come down the stairs first thing. Two soft leather cases with brass buckles, filled to bursting and leaned up against the wall.

Mom does not pack light. She is a glamorous woman.

Dad and Mom are in the kitchen, their voices drifting through the lobby. It's a vast house, way too big for just three of us since Tommy moved out. Even with Jamie in another wing, most of the rooms go unused—barely walked into except for the cleaners doing their rounds.

Dad says it doesn't matter. It's all about power. Projection. A businessman like him is expected to have a large estate and dozens of staff. Anything less and people will gossip. Respect will be lost.

So, fine. We have all these rooms and then use about six of them all together.

I wander into the kitchen: a huge, open plan room with an island and breakfast bar. There are sofas gathered around a wall-mounted screen at one end, where Dad and Jamie sometimes eat breakfast and mutter over the news. Even the fruit bowl on the counter is working overtime, groaning under the weight of perfect, waxed green apples and ripe peaches and plums.

There is too much fruit in this kitchen for this family to possibly eat. Especially once Dad and Mom set off after we leave for the doctor. I chew on my lip as I snatch up a banana, making a mental note to take some fruit pickings to the goats we keep at the back of the grounds.

No sense wasting good food. And besides, who'll be here to stop me? Jamie? He hates waste just as much as I do.

"You've got your judging frown on." Mom dips her spoon into a bowl of yogurt and honey. She folds it over and over, mixing it in, but never lifts the spoon to her berry red lips.

"This is my resting bitch face." I glance at her, but she doesn't smile. Mom is not a fan of mornings. She droops over the breakfast bar, already perfectly made up and dressed in a floaty silk blouse. Her platinum blonde hair rests in bouncy curls above her shoulders, far more lively than the rest of her.

Dad and Jamie look perkier, no doubt both having been awake for hours already. They're in dark suits and crisp white shirts, leaning against the counters. Dad winks at me as I slide onto a stool, but it's Jamie I smirk at as I peel my banana.

He takes a bite of his toast, studiously ignoring me.

Mom sighs tragically and drops her spoon into the bowl, dusting her hands like she's been tilling soil, not yogurt and honey.

"Are you ready yet, Carrick?"

Dad nods, a mostly full coffee mug pressed to his mouth. He grunts, chugging the coffee down, and slides his phone off the kitchen countertop. A few taps and it makes the whooshing sound of a message sending.

Probably super important. Millions of dollars at stake. Dad slides his phone into his pocket without another thought.

"Be good for Jamie." He ruffles my hair, and I smirk at the man in question over the tip of my banana.

"Oh, I will."

Dad scoffs and breaks off half the yellow fruit, then shoves it in his mouth. "Not too good," he says through the mouthful. "We have cameras, remember."

I roll my eyes at the reminder, but my mood lifts straight back up when I see how Jamie's cheeks have flushed red. That's the beauty of redheads: his every emotion is broadcast to the world.

I love making him glow like a little lava lamp. And he lets me push him so much further when Dad's not around.

Maybe this week will be fun after all. I pop the rest of the banana in my mouth and chew.

"Have a wonderful week, Francesca."

I wince at my full name as Mom kisses the crown of my head. Her perfume envelopes me for a second, and moisture brims in my eyes.

I blink hard. Where the hell did that come from? They're going away on business for a week, not moving to Mars. Even so, there's a lump in my throat as I watch their backs disappear through the doorway.

"They'll be back before you know it." Jamie's voice is soft across the kitchen. "And I'll take good care of you until then."

I bite the inside of my cheek and toy with my coffee mug handle.

"I'm a grown woman. Not a houseplant." He starts to say something else, but I slide off my stool and talk over him. "Let me know when you want to leave."

Because I can't even go to the doctor's alone.

Damn, I'm in a spitting bad mood this morning.

* * *

"Seat belt on."

Jamie lowers into the driver's seat, closing the door with a thump. I bite my tongue to keep from snarling at him—I'm twenty-two years old, damn it. I know to put my belt on.

His eyes find mine in the rear view mirror, and he frowns when he sees the angry set to my mouth. Whatever. I'm not responsible for everyone else's feelings, one hundred percent of the time. I'm entitled to be pissed off, and I tell myself so as I turn my head and look out the window instead.

The estate grounds roll past outside: manicured lawns, pale

stone statues and trees dressed in bright spring blossoms. A peacock struts through a flowerbed, his tail feathers swaying with each cocky little step.

I suck my teeth and smooth my dress over my legs. I've got leggings on, of course, covering the worst of my scars, but the morning sun is already beating down on the metal of the car and the extra layer makes my knees sweat.

Jamie interrupts my sour inner monologue, his rich voice carrying from the front of the car.

"Anything else on the schedule this week?"

I huff. "As if you wouldn't know."

I don't come or go from the estate without Jamie as an escort. A bodyguard. Glued to my side and constantly watching for the same men who hurt me all those years ago.

He's protecting me. Keeping me safe. I know that.

Doesn't mean I don't wish he'd leave me the hell alone sometimes.

"You are in a piss poor mood today, you know that?"

I shrug, staring out the window. He's not wrong.

"Everyone's moody sometimes."

"Sure."

"Like you, for example. Remember when that dry cleaner tore your suit?"

Jamie's hands clench around the steering wheel. I stifle a smile.

"That suit was a gift from your father."

"You were spitting mad."

"Wouldn't you be?"

I tug on a lock of his hair.

"No. Suits are lame."

Jamie huffs a laugh, shifting in his seat as we pull through the security gate. There are so many cameras pointing at the big iron gate and its little booth, you'd think we were gunning to host the president. I stick my tongue out at a camera, same as always, trying to figure which of Dad's men must be working today.

The car eases onto the street, and Jamie sobers up real fast. He doesn't mess around and tease out in public. He's on the job, one hundred percent focused. A redheaded terminator. After a while, I get bored with needling him and sit back, squinting at the street through the tinted, bulletproof glass.

Something's different. It's always lively out there, especially as we draw close to the city. There are always old men drinking and playing cards outside cafes; always music playing and dogs trotting past.

But today, there's a kind of spell on the streets. A weird urgency. The crowds are thicker than usual, spilling off the sidewalks into the road. They're all headed in the same direction, hips swinging and heads tossed back laughing, even though it's barely past breakfast.

Jamie curses just as his phone rings. He answers it, pressing a button on the steering wheel as Dad's voice fills the car. They chat about business—nothing interesting, just timings and logistics, and Jamie mentions a parade. Keeping one eye on the back of his head, I roll my window down half an inch.

We're supposed to keep the windows up. Sealed and secure. But Jamie's distracted, and it's like the spell on the city is sparking in my blood too. I want to know what it sounds like out there. What it smells like.

Strains of music wash into the car—not so loud that Jamie's onto me yet. There are pounding drums somewhere nearby, thumping out an intricate rhythm. The people walking down

208

the street fall into the same beat, their arms swinging and hips shaking. Then we round a corner and there's the faint tinkle of piano keys, spilling out an open bar doorway.

Jazz, blues, the steady pulse of club music. It all clashes and blends together in a medley of sound. And over it, the whoops and hollers of the crowd, calling to each other. We're still on the outskirts here, just turning close to the river. And we're driving the same way these people are walking, called towards something.

The car slows at a stoplight, right by a one-woman food stall. She's set up on the edge of the sidewalk, a great barbecue fire burning under a grill of roasting kebabs. Spiced meat and marinated pineapple sizzle on the grill, their scent wafting through the car window and making my stomach growl.

"Francesca," Jamie snaps. "Close your damn window."

I place my finger on the button, but I don't press it. Not yet. I suck in a whole lungful of delicious air first.

My window slides shut, controlled from the front. I glare at the back of Jamie's head.

"Don't be stupid," is all he says.

Stupid? Half an inch of open window, and the smell of street food?

Alert the church elders. Frankie O'Brien has truly gone buck wild.

About the Author

Kayla Wren is a British author who writes steamy New Adult romance. She loves Reverse Harem, Enemies-to-Lovers, and Forbidden Love tropes.

Kayla writes prickly men with hearts of gold, secretly-sexy geeks, and—best of all—she's ALWAYS had a thing for the villains.

You can connect with me on:
🌐 https://www.kaylawrenauthor.com
🔲 https://www.facebook.com/kaylawrenauthor
𝒶 https://www.bookbub.com/authors/kayla-wren

Subscribe to my newsletter:
✉ https://newsletter.kaylawrenauthor.com/beforethefall

Also by Kayla Wren

Lords of Summer
They tortured me all year at college.

Now I'm working the summer as their maid.

Lords of Summer is the first installment in the Year of the Harem collection.

Available now on Amazon.

Autumn Tricksters

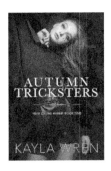

The circus can be deadly. It's smoke and mirrors; misfits and flames.

It's the place where tricksters come to play.

Autumn Tricksters is the second installment in the Year of the Harem collection.

Available now on Amazon.

Printed in Great Britain
by Amazon

51168370R00128